Once We Sang Like Other Men
Like Other Men

John MacKenna

NEW ISLAND

ONCE WE SANG LIKE OTHER MEN
First published in 2017 by
New Island Books
16 Priory Office Park
Stillorgan
Co. Dublin
Ireland

www.newisland.ie

Print ISBN: 978-1-84840-581-3
Epub ISBN: 978-1-84840-582-0
Mobi ISBN: 978-1-84840-583-7

Typeset by JVR Creative India
Cover Design by Karen Vaughan
Printed by TJ International Ltd, Padstow, Cornwall

New Island received financial assistance from The Arts Council (*An Chomhairle Ealaíon*), 70 Merrion Square, Dublin 2, Ireland.

10 9 8 7 6 5 4 3 2 1

For Katie and Mairenn Jacques and in memory of my dear friend Tom Hunt.

He now went up into the hills and summoned those he wanted.
So they came to him and he appointed twelve; they were to be his companions.

– Mark 3:13

Contents

Once We Sang Like Other Men   1

Resurrection   19

Words   41

Go Home to Your Friends   54

Sacred Heart   72

Say to Your Brother   88

The Angel Said   104

Buying and Selling   124

Absent Children   133

The Word   162

My Beloved Son   180

The Water of Life   200

Once We Sang Like Other Men   215

Acknowledgements   225

Once We Sang Like Other Men

This is where the sea stands still. This is where the moon comes to sleep on certain nights. This is where I sit, on the chair beside the boathouse. And this is where Laz sits, in his wheelchair, to the other side of the battered blue door that's never closed because there's nothing in the boathouse worth stealing, and I include the boat and the engine in that inventory of worthless insignificances.

One of the old men here chided me for painting the boathouse doors this shade of cobalt blue.

'It'll wash away,' he said. 'The sun and wind, summer and winter, gales and hail blowing in on it will see to that.'

'Maybe,' I said.

'Nothing more certain. You should've gone for something tougher. Why did you pick on that?'

'It's a colour I happen to like.'

'Liking something doesn't mean it works. Not always the same thing, liking and working. There isn't always a light at the end of the funnel.'

The old man shrugged and nodded and I nodded in return.

'But,' he drawled. 'I'm not here to upset the apple tart.'

After he had gone about his business, wandering slowly up the steep street, stopping now and again to analyse or criticise something else, Laz said quietly: 'Bastard.'

I built a small concrete patio for Laz's chair. It was rough and ready but the unevenness proved a boon. If I forgot to put the brake on the wheelchair, it didn't slide forward, didn't take off, ricketing down the slip and into the shallow water, as it used to do in the early days. Laz trying to wave his arms, swearing and grunting those animal grunts that I sometimes understood, pissing on himself when the cold water bit his feet and ankles and its sharp, stinging teeth came to rest around his knees. It always seemed to be winter when the chair went down the slip. But once I'd put in the concrete base, it didn't happen again. Instead, he'd sit in the wheelchair with the wheels locked in the rutted concrete, belt and braces stuff. Even when the spastic rages got him rocking and rolling, the worst that could happen was that he'd turn over the wheelchair and fall onto the sand on the dunes to the side of his platform.

In the early days, I used to say, 'You're like King Midas on your throne.'

I wasn't sure he knew who Midas was and it would have taken too long to explain, but he liked the idea of his wheelchair throne on its concrete podium.

In the bad days, when he gets under my skin, when there's nothing coming back and I'm wondering why I bothered bringing him here at all and why I ever felt the need to take some responsibility for the miserable life of a man who doesn't even know my name, I remind him that he's King Midas.

'Everything you touch turns to cold,' I laugh and he looks at me and I'm not sure if he knows I'm joking or whether he thinks he should be laughing but can't.

In the early years, there were some days when I really didn't want him near me. I'd wheel him down the pier and threaten to tip him in, wheelchair and all. I'd tell him I was going to stand on the pier and watch him drown in the twelve feet of clear water on the island side of the jetty. And I'd know, by the way his mouth would curl and his fists would tighten, that, even if he didn't understand everything, he at least got the gist of what I was threatening. Sometimes, on the really bad days, it was like I'd gone back and my mind hadn't yet found a place to rest or hide.

Now I wonder just how much he does or doesn't understand.

When we first came here, he could still talk. Not always lucidly, not so I could always have an articulate conversation with him, but he could communicate and he could understand most things. Even when he lost that little clarity of speech, when it was replaced by the grunting and coughing and gasping, he still knew what was going on. Once or twice, when I thought I was talking to the wind, he'd surprise me. I remember one morning in particular. I was wearing a shirt I treasured because, as I'd told him, she'd worn it on a night we drove across the desert in the pick-up truck, and he recognised it and gave me the thumbs up and his mouth opened in that horrific, broken-toothed grin that was intended to be warm but was as grotesque as an empty tomb.

Anyway, we've lived here together for twenty-four years, King Midas on his concrete and steel throne and Peter Pauper taking tourists out in the elegant and potentially lethal Treetop. I'm not sure who came up with my nickname but it stuck and I've developed a fondness for it.

In wintertime, this place is dead but that's the price you pay for being out of the rat race. That's why we chose this town. When I say we, I mean me. Laz had no say in the decision.

3

'Whither thou goest, there I will go, and where thou lodgest, I will lodge. Isn't that right, Laz?' I say and then I load him into the pick-up and off we go.

And he nods and smiles his terrifying smile and sometimes he gives me the thumbs up, other times he just sits there, eyes full of stones. If the weather is hot, I wedge the wheelchair in the back of the pick-up and sit him into it, fasten it and him with ropes, and off we go, out into the desert or up the coast, just rambling on wheels, me listening to the radio, him sitting in the sun, his cap pulled low over his eyes, sunglasses in place, looking out across the wilderness. Lord of all he surveys, Midas observing his sandy minions. The thing is, in summertime, once the temperature gets into the nineties, he stinks. It's something that never cleared up. I can't have him in the cab with me, even with the windows down: the smell is just too rancid, like something rotting fast, syrupy and sickly, the smell of cheap sweets going off in a shop window. Most of the time, when the weather isn't too hot, it's bearable but on hot days there's something about the mixture of diesel and slowly fading humanity that makes me retch. I've tried it once or twice and ended up on the side of the road, puking my guts up.

We came here in the spring when the place was deserted, temperatures in the twenties. I could haul my armchair out and sit in the middle of Main Street all day and not get run over. Some days I wouldn't be disturbed at all before lunchtime.

The first time I remember hearing of Laz, he was supposed to be dead. It was just before the Captain hit the headlines. We were sixty or seventy miles from the town where Laz and his sisters lived. The sisters had been to a few of the Captain's rallies; I think he knew them from way back. Only afterwards did I realise that they wanted to be on the road with him, they wanted to be at the heart of it all but of course they weren't.

They were like so many other hangers-on, looking for approval by association. At least no one could say that of me.

Anyway, we got the call and we set off in the pick-up, the Captain and Katy and me. I was driving. I was always driving. All I remember of the journey is the dirt roads and the Captain urging me to get there as fast as I could.

'I'm pushing this heap of shit to the limit,' I said. 'I can't go any faster. If we hit a hump, it'll rip off the exhaust.'

'Just do your best,' he said.

Typical. He'd never say, Come on, put your bloody boot down. It was, Do your best or Do whatever you can do, and the words were always spoken very calmly.

Sometimes I wanted to hit him when he did that. I'd feel I was being manipulated. But mostly I just made the extra effort because I wanted to do what I felt he needed doing.

So there we were, the three of us on this twisting road, in a pick-up with a dodgy fourth and heat like hell. And I knew the Captain wanted to get there as quickly as possible. I could feel the electricity coming off him and, occasionally, when I'd catch his reflection in the rear-view mirror, I'd catch those blue eyes staring straight ahead, as if they were willing us to be there more quickly than was possible.

The flies are what I remember about the little back bedroom in the house, that and the smell of burning joss sticks, put there to drown the other smells of shit and piss and decomposition. But all the two sisters seemed interested in was the Captain. It was like he'd come there for a party or to dinner or something. It wasn't like their brother had died. I don't think they'd have been worried had the Captain not even gone in to see Laz's body. They made coffee for us and they wanted us to eat after the long journey; there was plenty of food. This was, after all, a wake. They talked to the Captain, all the time; they talked to me, some of the time. They ignored Katy, as though she had no right to be there. Or perhaps they were jealous of her. I don't know.

I was never quite clear about what exactly happened in that room; there was no proper explanation from the Captain. Katy and myself were out in the laneway that ran behind the row of little houses that made up the street where Laz and his sisters lived. It was hot and humid in the house and we'd been sitting in the pick-up cab for the guts of two hours. We just wanted air and shelter from the sun and to be well away from this pair of intense and peculiar women.

We heard the noise long before we knew its cause. At first I thought someone else had died. Over the years, I've seen that happen at funerals and weddings and wakes and at the Captain's meetings. Someone becomes overwrought, someone says something that dredges stuff up, someone with a leaky ticker keels over. It happens. And I thought it had happened again. That was my first thought. But there was something about the way people were running in and out through the back gate, calling neighbours from down the lane, something about the tone of their voices – hysteria tempered with awe.

Another thing I'd learned over the years was how to read the mood of a crowd. It's something I needed to know, once our meetings began to get bigger and were infiltrated by shit-stirrers. Half a dozen troublemakers can do a lot of damage if they swing a crowd. Alternatively, they sometimes need rescuing if they misread the moment. Obviously we didn't want, and, equally, we couldn't afford, to have someone lynched at one of our meetings.

Anyway, there was something about those sounds, something about the way people wanted to be close to the wake house and, at the same time, wanted others to experience whatever it was they were experiencing. So I pushed my way through the garden gate. It was like a circus in the courtyard: people throwing themselves on the ground, tearing their hair, praising God, screaming incoherently. I never had much time for that kind of thing and neither, I know, did the Captain.

But, as I say, I have no idea what happened in that little room in that cramped house. I don't know if Laz was really dead. It's unlikely. I suspect he was in a coma and, by chance or the Captain's willpower, he came back from that state to a state of relative vigour, which isn't hard when everyone has you slated as dead. When it comes to vitality, anything is everything when you're dead.

By the time I got inside, Laz was sitting in a chair in the kitchen, looking like death warmed up but obviously breathing. People were giving him a wide berth but they were crowding around the Captain, wanting to touch him and to be touched by him, more of that fame by association stuff.

It was after midnight before I managed to edge the pick-up down the lane behind the house and get Katy and the Captain out of there. People were still crowding through the front door, not really knowing what they wanted but wanting it anyway. The last thing I saw, through the open kitchen window, was Laz still sitting in his chair, still looking like dried puke.

We were driving the desolate, arid road, twenty miles out of that town, a full moon saturating the yellow desert to our right and left, Katy and the Captain and me. And he had this serene look that always shrouded him after something significant had happened. Katy was sitting between us; the radio was playing very low, Crystal Gayle was singing 'Crying in the Rain' or something like that, a song that was oozing heartbreak. No one was really listening to the music and no one was saying anything, just this low, weeping melody and the steady murmur of the engine and even that seemed to be running lower than usual. It was like the moonlight had damped everything down, making us afraid to speak. And then somewhere, in the middle of nowhere, the Captain asked me to pull over the pick-up.

He got out and walked fifty yards, through the rubbish-strewn sand at the roadside, out to where the ground was softer and cleaner. I followed. Behind me I could hear the whispering music. I knew Katy was sitting on the step of the pick-up, smoking. I could smell the sweet tobacco in the heavy night air.

I caught up with the Captain and we walked together in silence. And then he stopped and stood looking back the way we'd come.

I knew he was thinking about what had happened.

'It'll change things, won't it?' I asked.

He nodded.

'This was the big one?'

He nodded again.

'There's no turning back now,' he said. 'No going back.'

We both knew it.

That was the last totally quiet time we had, standing out there in the desert under a big blue moon, two men looking at the sky, the night air warm and calm, the smell of cigarette smoke, two men listening to the silence, and behind them a woman sitting on the step of a pick-up, watching.

It was eighteen months later, weeks after the Captain's death, that I found myself back driving that same road, this time on my own. I decided, on an impulse, to swing by the town where Laz and his sisters lived. It wasn't hard to find their house, not in the five-street, one-river assortment that was their dark little community.

Laz wasn't doing well. I found him sitting in a wheelchair outside his front door. His skin was still the same sick colour but he looked a lot grubbier and more than eighteen months older. He had a begging bowl beside him and round his neck someone had hung a cardboard sign that read 'Where there's life keep life'.

I parked up the street and walked back past him. He didn't raise his head, didn't acknowledge me. He didn't seem, even, to be awake. Martha, his older sister, was inside the house. The other sister was nowhere to be seen. All she could talk about was how Laz hadn't really appreciated the second chance, how he'd been drinking too much and had fallen and broken his hip, how he didn't seem to have any real gratitude for the chance he'd been given and how anyone else would have taken the opportunity to make something of themselves.

I'm not an impulsive person. Twice in my life I've done impulsive things. The first time was when I packed a bag, walked out on my wife and kids, left my job and hit the road to follow the Captain. Goodbye was all she wrote.

The second time was that day. I manhandled Laz into the pick-up cab, hoisted his wheelchair into the back, propped the cardboard sign on the windowsill of his sisters' house and drove away through the pouring rain.

He still had a reasonable facility with words back then, on good days.

'Thank you,' he said. I could barely understand him. At first I thought he'd had a stroke but then I realised his teeth had all been broken.

'That's okay. What happened to your teeth?' I asked, expecting him to tell me he'd fallen and smashed them.

'Sisters,' he said.

'Sorry?'

'Broke them.'

'What are you talking about?'

'More money.'

'You're telling me your sisters broke your teeth so you could get more money?'

He nodded. There were tears in his eyes. I never saw him cry again.

We stayed in a cheap hotel that night. I rang Martha and told her Laz was with me.

'How are we supposed to live?' she asked.

I said nothing.

'Laz was my life,' she said.

I looked at him, sitting in the bath in our hotel room, covered in sores.

'Get a fucking job,' I said and hung up.

And, three weeks later, having wandered in and out of towns and villages along the coast, we ended up here.

I don't resent Laz. I don't ever take him down the pier now and threaten to throw him in, not even as a joke, which I know you'll say is big of me.

Mostly he's just here, but occasionally I think of him as the price I'm paying for the things I've done. As if I chose to bring him here as a living reminder of the mistakes I've made and the failure I've been. A punishment for walking out on my family, for not coming up to the mark with the Captain, for the way I let things fall apart.

Not that our life is a misery – far from it. We do all right. I take tourists fishing. Laz sits here and watches. Like I say, I don't know what he hears or how much he takes in but sometimes, even still, he'll surprise me.

There are nights when I talk to him about the old days. About his life and about mine and about where we might go someday, about having money, about comfort. I like to imagine that he still can daydream. I can't, not daydream, but I think he can. I'm never certain about how much he understands of the things I tell him but I have a sense that whatever he understands, he believes. Maybe he's just gullible and that's why he believed he was dead or, worse still, that's why he believed he was alive again.

One evening, a couple of months back, we were sitting outside the boat shed and the moon's sister was sleeping in the sea and he spoke, very quietly and slowly and clearly.

'Dead was how I wanted to be.'

I didn't imagine it. He said it. And then he was gone again, back to his grunting and sighing and silence.

I love being out in the boat, my boat. Just here, just beyond the breakwater. Not with tourists but on my own, without even a line over the side, listening to the evening birds, waiting for the moon to nudge above the hills, keeping a not too distant eye on Laz on his throne but still out here alone.

Sometimes I dream, not often but sometimes. And always the dream is the same one – of home. Funny how that word will always ring with emotion, isn't it?

Home. I say it, I remember it, I feel it.

If I say home, what's the first thing that comes into your mind?

For me it's the shore.

That expanse of sand, not like the stony slopes here. How it stretches away into the distance, north and south, and how it reaches out, westward, for the blue sky and the lost horizon and the sinking sun. And at the point where the sand meets the town road is my boathouse. Was my boathouse? I have no idea if it's still there. I haven't seen it in twenty-seven years.

That's where two of the kids were conceived, the first two. Warm summer nights when the sun had barely gone over one edge of the world before it was climbing out of the other. Too much wine, hardly enough time, too much optimism.

I can see the big double doors open and feel the shade inside that high, wide building and the almost-living smell of timber and the smiling feel of sunlight and the bracing scents of tar and canvas and oil. I still remember the bustle of the kids playing and the gentle wash of the waves at high tide and the chiming laughter. Not the drunken laughter you get on the streets here on a Saturday night. The laughter that rang there was children's laughter; nothing edgy about it, no threat behind its peals.

That's what I find myself listening for when adults laugh – the darkness, the cynicism, the uncertainty or the cruelty. Laz never laughs anymore. It's like he left it behind him along the way. I suppose I did, too. Sometimes when I've been drinking, I laugh but it's as if I'm not really laughing at all. I hear through it and can't ignore what lies beneath it. I can't ignore the other things I'm remembering. Children are unselfconscious; they're wrapped in their own world and, at the same time, they're open to everything. Reticence removes so many possibilities.

Across the road from the boathouse was my family home. It had a big porch that ran its length, grinning out across the sea. And on those summer nights, I'd glance up from whatever I was doing and I'd see the lighted windows, shining, the inside lights strengthening as the darkness outside deepened. They were like joyful eyes saying, Welcome, welcome.

Almost always, there was someone sitting there – my wife, one of the kids, a friend, a neighbour, sometimes my brother James, playing the mouth organ, the sad sound of that music flowing like a dark stream into the night sea. But I never resented the sound; it seemed as much and as right a part of the place as the children's laughter or my wife's warm smile.

That's how I remember some of those evenings. Me fiddling with a boat engine, the kids on the strand, James and my wife sitting on the porch, the music trickling across the road, and one of the other fishermen, or a man from the village, sitting on the bench at the boathouse door, smoking and talking quietly to me. Someone smiling; darkness creeping up like a big grey cat, soft and easy; the house lights growing stronger and the moon climbing out of the sea.

Home.

After the Captain's shooting and everything that followed, we were paralysed. Not so much by his death – things had reached a stage where that was almost inevitable. The publicity that followed the Laz affair was the step that took us to a place from which there was no going back and the Captain seemed to embrace that inevitability. And, once he'd been murdered, there were journalists and photographers and news reporters everywhere, coming up like crabs from the night sand. As if they smelled something, as if the Captain's death wasn't enough and there had to be something else that needed unravelling, some secret that had to be told. In the beginning I thought they actually knew something and that some piece of information had leaked out. Later, I realised that these people work on the basis that there's always something untold and, if they can't find it, they'll concoct it.

I still live in dread of one of them turning up. There'll always be a reason. In the beginning it was the story itself, then it was the first anniversary; now it's coming up on the twenty-fifth and I'll be looking over my shoulder again, just in case. In case someone has spoken, in case they track me down…in case.

The strange thing is, very often when you get to the heart of something momentous, the truth is banal. It's as if the blood looks less red, more black. There's no great energy from a dead body. It just loses its colour and its power and its possibility. It's as simple and ordinary as that. Mundane. The things that might be of interest to others are the things I'd never talk about.

So, that's how it was with us after the Captain's slaughter. Shock, then panic, then hope, then self-preservation.

The killing was the easy part, all done and dusted in short order, as clean as these things can be. He wasn't the only one to die; the country was in a state of chaos. That's how they got away with it: people believed what they were told. Hard to believe it now but that's how it was.

The panic was the worst part. We had no sense of history being made or a chapter ending or any of that stuff. Just his body laid out, his beard knotted with vomit and blood and spit. His eyes looking mad but it might have been the strip lighting in the hospital morgue. That's the bizarre thing. After they'd ambushed him, they actually took him from the roadside to the hospital to have his death validated, red tape and certificates in the midst of mayhem.

And I remember us all standing around his body in the morgue, not sure what we should be doing, waiting for who knows what – for him to do something? Probably. Expecting the truth to be something other than it is, expecting a miracle. Watching for his chest to start rising and falling again but of course it didn't. And, after a very short time, we realised it never would, so we put him in a box and took him away.

Five of us carried that box down the long hospital corridor. It was awkward, not enough room, scraping the blue-grey paint from the walls, our fingers caught and bloodied between the edges and the door frames. The box should have been on a gurney but we didn't have the patience to find one. We were too nervous, too terrified. I kept waiting for the clatter of soldiers' boots on the lino. I didn't doubt they'd shoot us there and then and mop our blood from the floor. That's how I pictured it happening, five bodies piled in a hospital corridor, fallen across a box that held a sixth.

But they didn't. I suppose they reckoned they didn't have to. I suppose they were right. That they could sense the fight had gone out of our bellies. We were lost, we didn't even really know what we were doing or where we were going or what we should do next. We were used to following. I'm not sure any of us was cut out to be a leader.

Outside the hospital, in the parking lot, some hangers-on, those who were deluded enough or sad enough to think something might happen, were waiting in the blinding sunlight. And, when they saw us, a sound rose from them, a haze of weeping and screaming and moaning. I can't stand that racket at the best of times but this was all the more frightening because it was calling attention to us. The sound was like saws running in the hot afternoon, mixed with the ambulance sirens coming and going in the hospital yard. It all made me jumpy. I just wanted to get out of there.

James and one of the others were in the front of this Ford Transit we had at the time. We slid the box into the back and I went up to the cab.

'Get it fucking moving,' I said. 'Get out of here before they start shooting.'

There were snipers on the roofs of each of the three hospital wings. We were sitting ducks. All it needed was one jumpy hero up there and we'd all have been done for.

I swung into the cab, Katy got in beside me. I had the engine running, my foot on the accelerator, itching to go.

'Why the fuck don't they drive?'

Katy shrugged.

I got out and walked up to the van, afraid to run, afraid all the time, of everything.

'What's the hold up?'

'I'm waiting for the others to get into the car. They're at the other end of the parking lot. John's driving them.'

'They'll catch up.'

'They may not. They could get cut off.'

I nodded and walked back to the pick-up, watching all the time for a movement on the roof, the wink of a rifle being lifted, the stirring of an arm, anything.

'What's the trouble?' Katy asked.

'Waiting for the car to come round.'

'There you go,' she smiled.

She often said that.

And then the transit was moving, the car swinging into its wake. I angled the pick-up behind the car and off we drove. No heroics, just a bunch of shit-scared people.

Most evenings I try to do the crossword. I sit here and puzzle it out and, occasionally, when I crack all the clues, I feel better about myself. Isn't that stupid? I mean, what are words? They're just vehicles that carry things around. They carry information in the newspaper. They carry directions. They carry worn-out emotions. And sometimes we take them seriously and sometimes we take them for granted.

We took the Captain's words seriously.

But when people are gone, sometimes all you're left with are words and memories and perhaps some photographs. Photographs are incidental and artificial. And the memories are subjective. The words are really the closest thing to truth that remain, so you go back to them, you weigh them and look for things in them, things that you value.

That night, after we'd taken the Captain's body from the hospital, we brought it back to a house where we'd all been staying. It belonged to a friend of a friend of someone. It was a big house in the suburbs and there were a lot of people there but we still weren't sure how safe we were or if the house was known to the army or whether we'd been followed.

Katy had taken the Captain's father to another house, in another part of the suburbs. We didn't want him getting caught up in whatever might happen; he'd been through enough. We still half-expected the worst, still half-believed we were of some consequence, though we weren't.

We had no plans; we didn't even know where we might bury him. Some people wanted a big funeral, a last Fuck You to the army. But the more we talked, the more we realised that was just what the government would want, an excuse to round us all up and put us away for good. We were already isolated; there was no real support left for the cause, if there ever had been. We'd be twenty or thirty people behind a hearse, walking into the open doors of a prison or into our own open graves.

We sat with his corpse for a couple of hours, some drinking, some not, trying to maintain tradition. The longer the night went on, the more we understood how isolated we were and how none of us had the slightest idea how to survive what was happening, much less how we might come out of this with any semblance of a political focus. I have no memory of who first came up with the idea. If I say it wasn't me, it sounds like I'm washing my hands of what happened, but I'm not. If that were the case, I wouldn't have stayed with it all the way to the end; I'd have walked away and left it to someone else or put my foot down and insisted it should never happen.

You have to recognise that those were not ordinary times. It's impossible, I think, for anyone who wasn't there to understand how we lived, how full we were of expectation and optimism and belief when he spoke and how petrified we were when he was gone, especially in the hours and days after his death. We had nothing left to live for, no sure direction, no clear faith and, worst of all, no hope.

We were used to living on the run but we believed the Captain knew where it was we were running to and that made the living from hand to mouth, the constant looking over our shoulders bearable, exciting even. We always believed he'd have another idea, manage another ruse, get us out of one last tight corner. But this time it was clear that he hadn't. And yet there was some faint, indelible residue of possibility, some place inside us where an aspiration lived on.

But you needed to be there, to have lived and travelled and eaten and listened and sang and laughed with him, to understand how we felt and what he meant to us.

Whether it was exhaustion or a desperate need for optimism, whether it was the wine or whether it was an ingrained belief or whether it was loss – whatever it was, sometime that night we took the Captain's body and put it in the Transit. And then we crowded into the pick-up and the car and the Transit and we drove out into the desert, to a relatively safe house we sometimes used when we needed peace and quiet. And we stayed there for what seemed like a long time.

And, slowly, what we had done began to sink in and we were horrified, guilt-ridden, and the unspoken blame began. We dared not look at each other. Discussing it was never an issue because we couldn't. Two of us buried what was left of the Captain in the desert. No words, no ceremony, no songs, no poetry, just an act of necessity.

Matt and Andy were the first to leave. I woke one morning and they were gone. Within a week the rest had scattered. I was the last to go. I wanted to say or do something to bring things to a close; I felt I owed him that. So I went down, just as the sun was rising on my last day at the house, and stood at the spot where we had buried him. We'd put four large stones in a line along the lie of the grave. I took them and hurled them as far as I could across the red morning sand, one towards each of the compass points so that, even if we wanted to, we could never find his grave again.

And then I drove for three days, stopping only to fill the petrol tank, living on coffee, driving without any sleep. On the third night, on the outskirts of some one-horse town, I thought I saw the Captain walking on the hard shoulder and my heart sang and I could feel the blood rushing in my ears and I slowed the pick-up and stopped but of course there was no one there. I was hallucinating, I needed sleep. So I pulled the pick-up over and I closed my eyes and I slept for thirteen hours and then I got on with the rest of my life.

Resurrection

i

It was the morning of the last day of February when the man at the other end of the phone told Miriam her husband was dead.

'There's no comfortable way for me to put this or for you to hear it,' he said. 'Your husband's body was found yesterday afternoon. No matter how I say it, it doesn't make it any easier for you. I'm sorry to be the one.'

Miriam took a deep breath. There were questions she needed to ask but they were beyond her for now, so she did the practical thing. She asked for the caller's name and a telephone number.

'It must be what, three in the morning – where you are? It's just after eight here; it's still dark outside.'

'Yes ma'am,' the soft Canadian inflection.

'So you won't want me calling you back in an hour.'

'This is a police station. I'll be on duty till eight but my colleagues can assist you any time.'

'Right.'

'Again, I'm sorry.'

Miriam found herself wondering about the policeman, about his age. He sounded young but it was more likely he was in his late thirties or forties, that he'd have some experience of this kind of thing.

'Do you have someone there with you?' he asked.

'Yes, Charlie, my son – he's here.'

'He's an adult?' He put the emphasis on the second syllable.

'No, he's six. But my sister will come.'

'That's good, ma'am. You call her and then you call us back when the time is right for you.'

'Yes.' She hesitated. 'How did it happen?'

'Looks like it was a natural passing. We need to wait for results. But there was no sign of anything untoward.'

'What a strange word,' Miriam said.

'I beg your pardon?'

'Untoward – it's a strange word.'

'Yes, ma'am. I guess it is.'

'If I call back in an hour or two, you'll still be there?'

'I'll still be here.'

'Thank you.'

'I truly am sorry.'

'Yes.'

Putting down the phone, she stood for a moment, not thinking, staring into the shadows of the hallway, and then, picking it up again, she rang her sister.

Suzann spoke to the Canadian policeman and to the embassy and to the travel agent and then rang their brother and arranged for him to travel with Miriam. She contacted the undertaker and the Department of Foreign Affairs and made coffee and lunch. She talked a little about Bart but not too much and then took Bart's photograph from the sitting-room mantelpiece and put it on the kitchen table, where they could see it when they felt the need to see it. Suzann organised everything without it being obvious and she listened to her sister and hugged her and smiled that smile that made Miriam believe things would be all right, in spite of everything. And, the following morning, when Miriam and Michael left for the airport, Suzann stood with Charlie and waved them goodbye.

ii

'Where's Mammy?'

It was late on the first evening of March.

Charlie was sitting at the kitchen table, swinging his legs and trying to kick off his damp runners without opening the laces.

'She's on her way to Canada,' Suzann said.

'Is Uncle Michael gone with her?'

'Yes.'

'How will they get there?'

'They're flying.'

'In an aeroplane?'

'Yes.' Suzann smiled.

'Angels can fly without aeroplanes. They have shiny, bright wings, brighter than the sun. Feathery wings.'

'Do they?'

'Do you know any angel names?'

She shook her head.

'Are angels related to chickens?'

Suzann laughed out loud.

'You're a funny little man.'

The boy nodded and then opened his mouth, as though he was about to ask something else, took a deep breath and was silent for a moment.

Suzann stared through the kitchen window but she could see nothing beyond her other self, gaping back from the rain-pocked glass.

'Your mum and Uncle Michael are going to bring your daddy back home with them,' she said quietly.

The little boy perked up, loosening a shoe against the chair leg.

'When will he be home?'

'Next week.'

'When will it be next week?'

'Five sleeps away. Or six.'

'Which?'

'Six.'

'Is that why daddy's picture is on the table?'

Suzann turned and smiled at him.

'Yes Charlie, that's why. To remind us.'

'To remind us that Daddy is coming home, so that we won't forget and go out and not remember to leave a key? We did that once.'

Suzann nodded.

'Can I stay up when he comes home? Will he collect me from school?'

'We'll see.'

'I don't like that photograph,' the boy said, holding the framed picture in both hands.

'Don't you? Why not?'

'I don't like the big rocks behind Daddy. They could fall on him.'

'Not in the photograph.'

'But sometime, and then he might die?'

iii

Miriam asked for the policeman by name, the one who had telephoned to tell her Bart was dead.

'He might not be here,' Michael whispered.

'I know that but he might. I want to see what he looks like.'

'Does it matter?'

Miriam shrugged.

They were sitting in a small office in the police station. Outside, old snow lay like twisted, unwashed dishcloths on the sills of the barred windows. Inside, the faded room smelled of steaming coffee and damp carpet.

A tall man stepped through the open doorway. Michael stood up and shook his hand.

'This is my sister. This is Miriam.'

'Steve Mallett,' the man said. 'I spoke with you on the phone.'

'I wondered how old you'd be,' Miriam said quietly.

'Probably not as old as I feel today.'

They sat, the three of them, and the policeman answered Michael's questions. It looked like Bart had died of a heart attack; they'd know for sure in a couple of hours but they weren't looking for anyone else in connection with his death.

'So this is what it means,' Miriam said. 'When you hear that phrase on the news.'

'This is what it means,' the policeman said.

'Can we see Bart?'

'Yes, of course. A car will take you to the hospital.'

'And he's, you know, he's okay?'

'He's okay.' The policeman smiled a reassuring smile.

'Who found him?'

'Next-door neighbour – old-timer, lives thirty minutes from the cabin. He went to see if your husband needed anything; seems they had any arrangement about picking up supplies from town. He found him and called us. It's about two and a half hours from here to there at this time of year.'

'Where did this man find Bart?'

'He was sitting at his table, ma'am, looked like he'd been working there. I understand he was a writer?'

She nodded.

'He couldn't work at home, said he couldn't concentrate. Never did, always had to live in the places he was writing about.'

The policeman smiled again.

'How long had he been dead?' Miriam was surprised by the calmness of her voice.

'A day, maybe two, I believe. But it's pretty cold out there; the place was freezing. Nothing had happened to the remains.'

'Is it possible for us to go out to the cabin?'

Michael glanced at the policeman and he immediately nodded.

'Of course. Sometimes, people want to see where a loved one passed away. I understand that. I can have you taken out there first thing tomorrow morning. It's a long trip, just so you're prepared for that. And the cabin is pretty isolated but we can get you there, yeah, sure we can.'

'You're certain you really want to spend five hours travelling there and back?' Michael asked.

'Absolutely,' Miriam said. 'I need to see.'

'It'll be all right,' the policeman reassured them. 'Trust me, everything is fine, it's not a problem, not a problem at all. And it's very beautiful out there. That may be some consolation.'

iv

Suzann was sitting on the side of Charlie's bed.

'How many days is it now until next week?'

'Still six.'

'You said that already.'

'Yes but that was this morning. It's still the same day. But it'll be a new day soon. When you wake in the morning, it'll only be five days.'

The boy nodded.

24

'Have you said your prayers?'

'God bless Mammy and Daddy and Auntie Suzann and Uncle Michael and me. And everyone. Amen.'

'That's it?'

'When Mammy is here there's more but I think that's enough.'

'Okay.'

Suzann tucked the bedclothes under the boy's chin.

'You're as snug as a bug in a rug,' she smiled, tickling him.

He laughed and squirmed and laughed again.

'Daddy always brings me a present when he comes home.'

'I know.'

'I think this time he'll bring me an aeroplane like the one he'll be flying in.'

She nodded but said nothing.

'Tomorrow, can we paint a picture of an aeroplane for Daddy, a big picture? And I can give it to him when he brings me my present.'

'Of course we can.'

'I like painting in the daytime when the sun is out. You can see things better.'

'Yes you can.'

'Why are you crying?' the boy asked.

'I'm just sad. But I'm happy, too. Happy to be here with you.'

'Will you stop being sad when Mammy and Daddy and Uncle Michael come home?'

'I'm sure I will.'

'Can you be happy and sad together?'

v

'I'm sorry, I can't take you folks up there myself,' Steve Mallett said. 'But Officer Marsh is one of our best. She'll take care of you.'

They were standing outside the front door of the police station, the dark morning traffic slushing past them on the main street of the town.

'I guess everything will be finalised within forty-eight hours. I'll be talking to someone from your embassy this afternoon. Everything will be in place by the time you get back from the cabin.'

'Thank you,' Michael said. 'We appreciate all you've done.'

A patrol jeep eased out of a gateway to the side of the station.

'That's your ride,' the policeman said. 'I'll introduce you.'

Miriam and Michael followed him down the wet concrete steps.

A young, casually dressed woman climbed from the jeep and came to meet them.

'Dominique Marsh,' she smiled. 'I'm sorry about your husband.'

'Thank you.'

She shook Michael's hand.

'Real sorry.'

'Not sure if you folks want to talk or not on the ride out,' Dominique said.

They were clear of the town and, ahead of them, where the road arrowed into the horizon, mountains reared above a thick smear of evergreens. Closer to hand, barns and silos crouched beside farmhouses, their backs pitted against the bitter, churning winds.

'Some folks do. Some don't; people differ at times like this. I brought some coffee and bagels. Best we get out to the cabin and let you have time. We can stop off on the ride back, get something more substantial, if you feel like it. Everything is your call.'

'Thank you,' Michael said.

They drove on, across the snowbound farmland and then, mile by mile, the fences and farmhouses evaporated until they were speeding through a bottle of murky green forest, the low light shattering as it fell between the trees.

'How could he write up here?' Miriam asked. 'He told me it was bright and white and clear. This is darkness.'

'Forty-five minutes on we're into snowfields,' Dominique said. 'And then it's just stands of timber and an eternity of snow. It's everything you don't see here – white, bright, clear, fresh. And mostly just empty.'

'That's what his letters said.'

'How long had your husband been up here?'

'Since just after Christmas. Eight or nine weeks. He'd planned on staying till the end of summer.'

'He was a writer?'

'Yes.'

'A good one, I guess.'

'I think so.'

'That's it,' Dominique said, pointing into the wilderness ahead. 'That's the cabin. Just thought I should tell you that we're almost there.'

Michael leaned forward from the back seat and Miriam squinted into the rosy whiteness.

'To the left of that stand of trees.'

'I see the trees,' Miriam nodded.

As they drove, the cabin began to take a shape within the shadow of the coppice, a low and regular building and behind it what looked like a garage. Bart had told her, in his first letter, that he had bought a small car. It was a necessity out here. A small and simple house and a small and simple car, what else had she expected? Wherever he went, Bart chose to live austerely. He detested ostentation. Sometimes, she thought, he had no choice but to go; even their modest house seemed to hold echoes of affection for him.

As they swung off the roadway and onto a rough track, Miriam could clearly see the cabin now with its shuttered garage and, behind that, a woodshed precisely stacked with neatly sawn logs. The logs had come with the cabin, Miriam knew. Bart had told her. He wouldn't have had the patience for such orderliness.

She was thinking of Frost's lines about the woods and the frozen lake. Somewhere beyond that stand of trees, somewhere in a hollow in the snow she supposed, was a lake, ice-covered but breathing in the expectation of spring. Without that anticipation, how could anything or anyone go on?

Then, right away, she was overwhelmed by the enormity of what had happened. There were no tears. Instead the cold seemed infinitely colder and the emptiness of the landscape was immense, and the forlorn, the unlit windows of the cabin were deep, black holes that terrified her.

Michael coughed and only then did she realise that the jeep had come to a standstill and that Dominique was assiduously looking into the distance, allowing her the time to prepare herself.

'I'm sorry,' Miriam whispered. 'I was just thinking how beautiful it is out here. And how lonely.'

Dominique laid a gloved hand on her arm.

'I can go in with you or I can stay out here – whatever way you want it. It'll look just like any other room in any cabin, I promise you. I realise it'll mean much more to you but there's nothing to be afraid of.'

Michael put his hand on her shoulder.

'You okay, sis?'

She nodded, smiled and opened the jeep door.

Inside the cabin it was colder than she had expected, colder than outside, as if the wind had gathered every shaft of iciness and shut it up in the half-darkness of this functional room, dulling its light and congealing its coldness.

Michael stood in the shining doorway. Beyond him she could see Dominique just outside, listening and waiting, on duty. Miriam stood in the middle of the room and, closing her eyes, breathed slowly, deeply, searching for the moment of her husband's death, listening to the ice crack on the gutters, feeling the weak dusk from the small window lean uncertainly on her left hand. But she found nothing of Bart. What had she expected: that there'd be any more of him here than there was in the house they shared? That, secretly, this had become home to him.

Opening her eyes, she moved between the plain kitchen table, with its four sturdy chairs, and the small desk that faced a window filled with distant, drunken trees. Some notebooks sat, neat and silent, side-by-side on a flock of coffee rings. Two loose pages lay together, a pair of redundant wings, feathered with Bart's scrawl, lost now without the force that had made them fly.

She lifted the top sheet and read a list of things undone and groceries unordered.

The second page was tidier, lined and neatly written.

It's snowing here again tonight.

I hope it's snowing there, too.

I like the idea of you sleeping and snow falling outside your window.

I imagine myself standing at that window, looking out at the snow, then turning back to watch you sleep.

vi

On the morning of the day that Bart's body was due home, Suzann told Charlie about his father's death. They were sitting at the kitchen table, low sunlight streaming through the picture window. She said the usual things, the words she had heard others use when they spoke to children about death. She told him something terribly sad had happened, she reminded him of how much Bart loved him, she assured him that his father's love would never stop, just that it would be coming from a different place, about how Charlie would find his father's star in the sky and know he was always there.

'Stars are not people,' the boy said.

'They can remind us of people we loved.'

'What if two people pick the same star to remind them? Whose star is it then?'

Suzann smiled, relieved that this was the question he'd chosen to ask.

When Charlie's father came home, it was in an enormous wooden box and the box was left in the sitting room and people came and went and they kept stepping over Charlie where he was playing with his digger on the floor at the foot of the stairs. All those legs and all that talk and, from time to time, a hand reaching down from the sky to rub his head and, afterwards, the smell of perfume from his hair. And someone gave him money and he squashed it into the little pocket at the front of his jeans and thought for a minute about what he'd like to buy and wondered if his father had remembered to bring the aeroplane he'd promised. And then he went back to his work, digging blocks from the hall carpet and piling them on the first step of the stairs.

Charlie woke while it was still dark. He always woke in the darkness. He liked to wander around the house in the shadows from the landing light. At the foot of the stairs he stopped; there were voices in the kitchen, so he turned right, into the sitting room where his father was still keeping out of sight.

Putting his ear to the box, Charlie listened. His father was keeping very still, he was good at that. Charlie knew what he needed to do: he needed to surprise his father. He waited, silent, unmoving, counting to fifty, counting and waiting for longer than he'd ever done before. Then he knocked loudly on the side of the box inside which he believed his father was hiding, knocked and giggled because he suspected his father couldn't keep still for ever and he knew his father loved to hear him laugh; it made him laugh too.

Suzann was suddenly beside him, her arm across the boy's shoulder.

'What are you doing, little man?'

'Playing hide and seek with Daddy. I know where he's hiding. He's in the box. I can hear him.'

vii

'I'm tempted to pull the fucking lid off the coffin and slap his face,' Miriam said.

She and Suzann were standing in the back garden, drinking coffee, stooped against the black March wind. A few beaten daffodils huddled at the foot of a dividing wall.

Suzann looked again at the sheet of paper her sister had pulled from her jacket pocket.

'All it says is, I hope it's snowing there, too.'

'It rarely snows here. You know that, I know that, he knew that. This is not for me.'

'It's probably just a piece of a story, something he was working on. Notes. He was always leaving notes around the house. You said that yourself, ideas, bits and pieces. That's what writers do. I think.'

Miriam warmed her face in the steam from her coffee cup.

'His notes are on his laptop. I've read them. They have nothing to do with this. And anyway, there was an envelope, with the page.'

'Was it addressed to anyone?' Suzann asked quickly.

'No.'

'There you are then.'

'The page was sitting on the lip of the envelope, ready to be put inside.'

'You don't know that.'

'There was a roll of stamps beside it.'

'This is not a good time to come to these conclusions. This is not the time to decide stuff like this. Honestly it's not.'

'He was expecting some old guy to call. There was a grocery list beside it. He was going to address the bloody thing and have it posted. I know, Suzann. Don't tell me I'm not right. You always try to find the balance in things, but sometimes there is no balance. Sometimes life is totally unbalanced, it's dark, it's disingenuous, it's fucking twisted. The fact is – and I know this in my heart – he just hadn't got around to addressing the envelope. So fuck him.'

viii

Charlie was mesmerized by the priest who was to conduct his father's funeral service. He was a tall young man with a mop of brown hair and a smile that the six-year-old recognised as genuine.

He knelt by Charlie in the church and shook his hand and asked how he was.

Charlie said he was fine. He talked about Charlie's father the way Charlie did, as though the game of hide and seek which was going on would end when Charlie least expected it. He let Charlie light the taper from which the candles would be lit.

He asked if Charlie would like to come up and speak about his father from the altar during the service. The boy looked at the expanse of white marble he'd have to cross and shook his head. The priest showed him where to leave Bart's camera, when the time came to present the gifts of remembrance, on a small table with three of Bart's books, and then he said they'd talk later.

Watching the priest move along the front of the altar space, distributing the communion wafers, Charlie began to believe the marble wasn't so expansive after all.

And when the priest talked about death and life, he listened.

'If we believe in Jesus the Christ, then we believe in the promises he made. We not only believe, we trust. Jesus promised his disciples that he was the way, the truth and the life. We can find our way to that truth through Jesus' life. We can rediscover the joy in life by recognising that death is not the end. Jesus preached the resurrection and his disciples had their faith rewarded on Easter morning when, as the sun rose, they found a very real presence in the absence of Jesus from the tomb. We are four weeks from Easter, the rationale of life and death lies there. We have faith that we shall rise again and, as Paul tells us in I Corinthians: "For now we see through a glass, darkly; but then face to face." We believe, even better we know, that we will see Bart face to face again.'

The priest smiled at Charlie and Charlie smiled back. Glancing to his left, he saw that his mother's eyes were closed. To his right, Suzann was crying. She caught him watching her, took his hand and held it on her lap. Her hand was cold but her clothes were soft and they had a gentle smell of perfume that made him feel warm and wanted. He shifted slightly in his seat, moving closer to her.

ix

'If I could pity the bastard, I would, but I can't. If he'd died a day later, I'd never have known but he wouldn't, would he? That might have spared everyone.'

Miriam was standing at the sink, staring into the solid, sunless garden.

'Have you said anything to Michael?' Suzann asked.

'I have not! I don't want everyone to know what a fool I was. No one knows but me, you and her – whoever she is. I wonder if she's even heard that he's dead. I keep expecting the Canadian police to forward one of her letters to me. If they did, I'd have a name.'

'Well, it's been three weeks and they haven't. Surely that counts for something?'

'Most likely she lived somewhere in that godforsaken town, probably a waitress in the local caff or a fucking pole dancer. She'll have been close enough for him to get to. She'll know by now. They always do.'

Suzann came and stood by her sister. Together, they watched Charlie in the garden outside. He was kicking a ball into the wind, laughing each time it lifted above his head and landed at the other end of the lawn.

'He's taking it well,' Miriam said.

'Seems to be. I'm not sure how much of it has sunk in.'

'He knows Bart's dead, if that's what you mean.'

'Of course he does.'

Outside, the ball soared into the wind, bounced on the narrow lawn and disappeared into the neighbour's garden.

'Got it,' Suzann called.

Charlie could see the top of her head above the dividing wall.

'I'm going to throw it in to you. See if you can catch it.'

The bright, shining ball held in the wind and blew back into the next-door garden.

He could hear Suzann laughing.

'I wouldn't make much of a player, would I?' she called.

'Throw it again. Harder.'

She did and it bounced beside Charlie.

'Have you got it?'

'Yes.'

'Right. Coming over.'

Her face appeared above the wall and then she pulled herself up and sat on the narrow blocks.

'Humpty Dumpty sat on a wall,' she laughed, rocking puppet-like, backward and forward. 'Humpty Dumpty had a great fall.'

Suddenly she tumbled, all arms and legs, onto the lawn.

'All the king's horses and all the king's men couldn't put Humpty together again.'

Charlie came racing across the garden and jumped on her. Together they rolled, tickling and giggling in the cold grass, their arms about each other, hugging together against the hardness of the ground.

'How long are you going to stay with us?' Charlie asked quietly

'Till Easter, the week after Easter.'

'When is Easter?'

'Not next Sunday but the one after that. Ten days.'

'I like when you're here.'

'Thank you.' She hugged the small boy close to her. 'I'm going to buy you the biggest Easter egg you've ever seen. It'll take you a month to eat it.'

'And Daddy will bring me an egg.'

'Not this year, sweetheart.'

'Jesus came back. The man said Daddy will come back too. And he might bring an egg for me, if he can find one.'

x

'I took Bart's photograph off the mantelpiece,' Miriam said. 'I put it in Charlie's bedroom.'

'Why?'

'I thought it would be good for Charlie to have it there. As a reminder.'

'I'm not sure he likes that picture. He's afraid the rocks will fall on Bart. Anyway, the first thing he did every morning was to go into the sitting room and say hello.'

'Well now he can do it when he wakes. And last thing at night. And I don't have to see Bart staring at me when I'm watching telly. A win, win situation, isn't that what they call it? You only have to look at Charlie to see he's flying. He laughs all the time. He's happy, Suzann, that's the important part. I can deal with what Bart did. See no evil, speak no evil.'

'He wasn't an evil man.'

'If you say.'

'You know he wasn't.'

'You're not telling me that what he did was acceptable?'

'You have no idea what he did or if he did anything. A few words on a sheet of paper, a blank envelope, that doesn't amount to evil or anything remotely like it. This has to do with other things, Miriam, things about Bart's being away, and that's understandable but it does not make him an evil man. Just let it go with him. Give him the benefit of the doubt, or don't if you can't, but let it go.'

'Easy to say. If you want to know me, come and live with me. I feel totally humiliated and used and I do not want to see that dark, suntanned, self-satisfied face grinning down at me night after night. Charlie likes having the photograph in his room, whatever you say, so good for Charlie. Like I said, it's all win, win.'

xi

Only after his mother and aunt had tucked him in and read him a story and tickled and laughed with him and promised to help him in the morning to find the places where his eggs might be hidden, after they had kissed him goodnight and wished him sweet dreams and told him he was the best boy in the world and that they loved him more than anyone else, after they had switched on the soft bedside light and closed his door, did Charlie take his dinosaur clock from the shelf above his table, wind it and set the alarm.

xii

'I think I'm going to sell this place,' Miriam said.

She and Suzann were sprawled on the couch in the sitting room.

'Wouldn't Charlie miss his friends, the school, all that?'

'I don't mean to leave the town, just the house. I never liked it. The rooms are too small, too gloomy. Bart said it was big enough, which was easy for him, he was never here. Passing through between books. And women, it seems.'

'Charlie thinks Bart is coming back.'

'What?'

'He thinks he's coming home for Easter.'

'Shit, where did that come from?'

'I'm not sure. From what the priest said, I think.'

'What priest?'

'At the burial service.'

'What did he say?'

'Charlie thought he said Bart would be back at Easter, like Jesus.'

Miriam laughed out loud and then her eyes filled with tears.

'I'm sorry,' she said. 'I didn't mean to laugh. It's just another good reason to keep religion and children apart, fairytales and bullshit. Well at least the Easter Bunny will come. That much we can see to, that much will happen.'

37

xiii

Charlie dressed quickly by the light from the bedside lamp. It was five o'clock. He wasn't sure if that was very early or just early. He made no attempt to be quiet. It never crossed his mind that he should. He was too excited.

Downstairs, he didn't bother to look for his eggs. Instead, he wriggled clumsily into his jacket, zipped it up, pulled on his cap, opened the hall door and stepped into the melting yellow light outside.

xiv

Miriam woke to the darkness. Pressing her mobile phone, she squinted at the dim, scratched screen.

Bugger, she thought, forgot to charge it again.

Something after five but she couldn't decipher the minutes.

Turning back towards sleep, she considered for a moment the fact of Bart's death. She thought of him on that morning or afternoon or night when the end had come in the isolated cabin. It was like a nightmare to her now. But, in that moment, she allowed herself to forgive him whatever wrongs he might not have done. She imagined him recoiling from the bullets of pain inside his arm and the convulsive explosion in his chest. And she pitied him the terrible hurt of that moment. And then she slept.

xv

Suzann found him.

She had sensed, when he didn't come bounding into her bed at six o'clock with the egg she had left on his bedroom table, that something was wrong. She had gone into his room and then looked in on her sister's sleeping form before hurrying

38

downstairs. She saw, immediately, that his jacket and cap were missing from the low peg in the hallway.

Upstairs, she pulled on her jeans, a jumper and the jacket with the fur-trimmed hood; it would be cold outside, she knew that.

At the foot of the stairs, she dragged on her socks and jiggled into her boots.

In the street, the windscreen of her car was frozen. Splaying her hands, she pressed them hard against the glass until the ice began to melt in fingers and palms.

And then she was driving, swinging out through the wide and curving crescents of the estate, into the narrow street of the old town, past the voiceless yard of Charlie's school and sharply left onto the avenue, with its cortège of wintry trees, nodding mutely towards the ravenous gates of the graveyard.

Though she doubted Charlie had even noticed her car lights at the gate or heard her running feet on the gravelled path, he didn't seem at all surprised to see her. His knees were resting against the frozen mound of Bart's grave. His face looked pale and tired.

She knelt beside him, aware immediately of the cold and damp seeping through the knees of her jeans.

'I think Daddy will come soon,' Charlie said, nodding towards the eye of a railway bridge. Through it Suzann could see a vein of light against the edge of night.

'Maybe he will,' she said.

They hunkered closer, waiting for whatever it was they believed, separately or together, was about to happen.

'The sun is coming up,' Charlie whispered.

'So it is. Maybe the sun will blow the snow away.'

'There isn't any snow.'

His voice was sleepy and hoarse.

Suzann opened her coat and hugged him to her, taking his frozen hands in hers, letting his rigid frame fold against the warmth of her own.

'Let me tell you a secret,' she whispered. 'Sometimes it snows and people don't even know.'

Words

I love this bar. It's everything I ever dreamed about. I took my time with it. Stood over the architect when he was tooling around with his version of what he thought I needed, rather than listening to what it was I knew I wanted. I stood over the builder and reminded him of who was paying when he had these brilliant ideas for speeding the job up by cutting corners because there was another one in the offing down the street.

Some days, dealing with him was like meeting a nutcase armed with an Uzi, and some days it was like saying 'Give me the gun' and hoping he'd hand it over without shooting.

'Matt, you're a hard man,' he'd smile.

'Paul, you're a fucking Legolander,' I'd say and the two of us would laugh and he'd down his mug of tea and get back to doing what it was I wanted him to do.

I stood over the plasterer when he tried to put a smooth finish on the inside walls.

'That's not what I had in mind.'

Eventually he agreed to do as I asked, on condition that I didn't tell anyone who had been responsible for the plastering.

'I'd be laughed out of the place; it'll look like some not very clever, hung-over, half-blind first-year apprentice did it on a bad day. If I imagined anyone thought I'd finished a job that rough on purpose, I'd leave this town.'

'It's the way I want it.'

'I know that, you know that, but does the rest of the world know that? If you wanted a derelict building, you should have bought one. I hate this chic derelict shit.' He pronounced it 'chick'.

'My lips are sealed,' I said.

'They fucking better be,' he grunted, going back to the plastering, sighing and swearing and rolling his eyes.

And when the place was ready, I delayed the opening by a day, even though it was high-summer, tourist season, and I needed the money. I wanted the place to be mine, just mine, for that single day; to enjoy the fruits of what I'd been planning all these years. I spent that whole morning sitting in every seat in the barroom, walking about the place, leaning on the counter from both sides, running my hand over the rough, rutted walls and smiling because everything was just as I'd always imagined it would be. At one point a man knocked on the closed glass door, his family lined up behind him, and mimed that they needed food and drink.

I mouthed back *tomorrow* and they shrugged and slowly moved away and even that pleased me, the fact that they wanted to be in my bar, they didn't want to be three doors up or five doors down. They had seen what I'd created and they needed to have their slice of it. Or so I told myself.

I still get that feeling on these July mornings when I open the doors onto the heat-drenched pier and last night's smoke is sucked out by the spinning summer wind and today's work still hasn't begun. For those few minutes this place is mine alone again. I don't consider yesterday's takings, I don't think about today's responsibilities, I enjoy the pleasure of the moment. It's not something that comes easily or naturally to me, but I've learned to do it. Out of the corner of my eye I catch the passing shadow-people, hear the distant sounds of traffic and the less distant sound of the sea and I'm happy for now. Possibility is a small child at the top of a morning staircase.

And then the first of the new week's customers arrives, a dour-looking man with three days of beard and three nights of drinking behind him.

'Americano,' he says. 'Twice.'

I pour the hot sticky liquid and then pour it again.

He drinks quickly, emptying the first cup and then the second.

'That should steady the ship.'

'I hope so,' I say.

'Fucking and drinking. Lost the weekend.'

'Lucky man.'

'Doesn't feel like it. Same again.'

I pour two more coffees.

The man reaches into his jeans pocket and pulls out a handful of cash and paper, hands me some money, and then searches through the wads of tattered paper, finally disengaging a sheet from the crumpled mess.

'This is for you,' he says.

I unfold the sheet. It's an invoice.

'You ordered the stone for the bones?' he says.

'Sorry?'

'The headstone. You ordered it?'

'Yes.'

'That's the damage.'

'Right.'

'Put it up on Friday. I was supposed to drop that off here on Friday evening but I got waylaid, well laid anyway. I can hardly walk. I'm shanghai'd. Dehydrated.'

I pour him a glass of water.

'Drink that.'

He does.

'You don't have to pay till you check it out but I couldn't go into work and tell the boss I hadn't delivered it.'

'Right.'

'I was shagging this woman on Friday night. She asked what I did for a living. I give the dead erections, I said. She kind of froze for a minute till I explained. Then I think she found it kinky. Didn't get away from her till this morning, so it must have done something for her.'

I nod.

He empties the tumbler of water and I refill it.

'The stone looks well?' I ask.

'It's straight. It'll stay up. A stone's a stone to me; it's work. I think I knew the old bugger.'

'Henry?'

'That was his name, so I read on the stone. I never knew him as anything other than Blue. He had an allotment out near my father's place. Often wondered where he got the name. Probably a porn reader in his day. We always steered clear of him as kids.'

'Why?'

'Dunno. Just did. He was odd.'

I nod.

'Pour me another two caffeines,' the man says. 'Then I'll hit the road.'

I pour the two coffees and put them on the counter.

'And he'd shout at us if we went near his allotment. We didn't have to go into it – anywhere within a mile of it and he'd start shouting,' the man adds, putting the money on the counter.

'Lots of people do that. Probably afraid you'd damage his vegetables and stuff.'

'Probably.'

The man drinks the first of the two coffees but slowly this time, seeming for once to savour it.

'I don't think I could live without alcohol, women and coffee,' he says. 'But if I had to drop one, I'd drop women. I love fucking them but they always want you to stay around afterwards. Or they want to stay around. And they expect you to say stuff, to talk all kinds of crap about feelings and affection when you just want to sleep or watch TV or go for a drink.'

I nod again, not because I agree but because really I have nothing to say to him on the subject.

'I suppose that's the way it is,' he says, as though that explains everything. He sips his coffee and something changes in his eyes. I can't be sure if it's a light going on or a light going out. 'Have you ever been in love with someone?'

'I suppose,' I say.

'It's different when you're in love; different from just shagging.'

I shrug. I'm not going to be drawn into this.

'I mean it's not that I want a woman hanging around me, not at all, not one that means nothing to me. But once or twice I fell in love. It's different then. You don't want to get pissed or to get them pissed. You want to do things, go to places, walk down a street on a Saturday afternoon and not give a shit about who's doing well in the league or who scored or any of that stuff. Do you know what I mean?'

I raise an eyebrow, hoping he'll take it as assent.

'It's like finding something new in something you thought was burnt out. It never lasts but it's good while it's there. For that couple of days or weeks you start to believe that your life might be different, that this might be the one thing that'll change it, pull it out of the rut it's been in for months or years, make you believe for a while that it doesn't have to be the way you thought it always would be. You start believing that just maybe you were wrong about life before, that there is a secret at the heart of it and you were just missing it every time.'

He pauses and drinks very slowly from the second cup on the counter.

'And then it just goes out, like a candle, and all you're left with is the smell of smoke and burning rubber.'

He is silent then.

I wash and dry the empty coffee cups and saucers and stack them under the counter. Then I check the beans in the coffee machine.

'Do you ever feel the dead around you when you're working?' I ask.

Now it's his turn to shrug, then he shakes his head.

'Nah. I don't think I'd do the job if I did. It'd be like carrying a hungry horse across a marsh. Not something you'd want to do in your right mind. Can't say I ever got any inkling of anything. Not once.'

'Right.'

'If you don't mind me asking, why did you pay to put a stone over Blue's grave?' He was staring straight at me, as though he expected me to lie and the only place he'd find the truth was in my face.

'He called here most nights.'

'I'm sure a lot of people do but you hardly go hearse-chasing when they empty their lungs.'

'To get something to eat. He'd come to the kitchen door. Sit on the back step. He'd never come in – even on rainy nights. Sometimes he wouldn't even stay – just take the food and be gone.'

'Doesn't explain it. Was he your father?'

I laugh.

'No. My father is safely buried a thousand miles away. Nothing so romantic.'

'Reminded you of your father then?'

'Not even that. Just a man.'

'How long'd you known him?'

'Six, seven, eight years maybe. Eight max. It's a pretty simple stone, nothing fancy, just a plain stone.'

'I know,' the man laughed. 'I put it up. But it'll still cost you.'

'Yes.'

'Where'd you get those words from, the ones on the stone?'

'He said them to me once.'

'Well fuck me, imagine that!'

He drinks some more of his coffee but he doesn't seem to want to leave. I know my answers haven't satisfied him.

'Just that most people wouldn't do that without a reason. Even for some old timer they knew. Got his face blown off by a shotgun I heard.'

'No,' I correct him quickly. 'He didn't. Rats did whatever damage was done to his face. He wasn't found for almost a week. The police thought at first that he'd been shot, but it turned out he died of natural causes.'

'You sure?'

I saw him shiver.

'Yes,' I say. 'Positive.'

'Fuck. Where was he found?'

'In the old bunker down past the bridge, past the allotments. Used to bring me fruit here in the autumn and onions and stuff, but then it got so he couldn't work his piece of ground anymore. That's what killed him.'

'What?' the man laughs. 'The onions or the fruit?'

He knows by my expression that I'm not amused and he stops laughing.

'Something he said to me, about two weeks before he died. We were sitting out on the back step,' I say and then I stop talking.

'And?'

'It doesn't matter.'

'Okay,' the man says quietly and he downs the last of his coffee. He realises he's said too much already. 'You check the stone out, in your own time, then you can pay the bill.'

'Sure.' I smile.

I don't feel any antipathy towards him. Don't feel anything at all about him. As far as I'm concerned, he's just someone passing through, a customer. A mouth but nothing worse. I'm well used to his type, used to listening and letting things go.

The man rises from his stool and then sits down again, looking me straight in the eye.

'Something happened one time,' he says.

'Yes?'

'Changed things. For me. Changed me, I suppose.'

'Right.'

'I was in the police force for a couple of years. I joined young, straight from school,' he said and then there was a long silence. For a couple of moments I thought that was it, that he had nothing further to add. But then he went on, slowly, deliberately. 'I was twenty-two, raw, still wet behind the ears. There was a murder in the town where I was stationed, young girl, late teens. Pair of thugs pulled her into a van, raped her, murdered her, dumped her body in a field. Some old guy saw it all, reported it. I was in the car that was sent out to investigate. The sergeant left me there, to secure the crime scene, while he put in a call to the district detectives. Then he rang me back, said it'd be a couple of hours before they'd arrive and I was to stay with the body. I'd been with bodies before, suicides and the like, but never for that long. I didn't like it out there in the middle of a moonlit field with a pretty young girl lying beside me. I kept thinking about what might have happened if I hadn't been there, rats, all that stuff. Strange what can happen in your fucking head in a couple of hours; the tricks your mind plays. You start hearing things, seeing things. Shadows start to move, noises take on a tones you've never heard before. It all starts to get to you. Well I know it started to get to me. Every time the wind blew and the grass moved, I imagined something scratching around the young girl's body, rats and mice, wild animals. I started thinking I was hearing something gnawing. Sweat was pouring out of me, even though it was an autumn night. She'd been dumped in the hollow of a field, out of sight of the road. It was five o'clock in the morning and I knew the murder squad wouldn't appear before daylight. I knew I was on my own and I was fucking petrified. Not by the dead girl but by what might happen to her. I was seeing things everywhere, shapes that might be something, in the shadows of the ditch, and I was convinced they were coming to move the body. I started talking out loud, to convince the shadows that I wasn't alone, to convince myself that I wasn't in danger of fucking everything up. The longer the night went on, the more it seemed to me that the darkness got darker. I know I got more and more terrified. By the time the light started to break and the sergeant got there, I knew I was finished being a policeman.

"'Just grabbed a bit of breakfast," he said. "You got on all right?"'

"'Yes," I said.'

"'Good man. Go and get yourself something to eat."'

'I didn't eat for two days, and a week after that I quit.'

The man stops talking as quickly as he's begun.

'You're still in the business, to an extent,' I say.

'Stones,' he says. 'Stones don't fuck your head up.'

And then he gets up, crosses the barroom and, without turning, waves from the door. I fold the invoice and put it in my shirt pocket.

It's the end of that week before I get to visit the cemetery. The stone is in place as he'd said. Commonplace, simple, just as I'd ordered, with the old man's name and date of death. Marking a life, if only by recording its end. Maybe that's all we can do or hope to have done for us. Maybe that's it. And the man has done a fine job, a really thorough one. Everything neat, no splashes of dropped cement, the ground has been left raked and seeded, the seeds about to strike, good work well finished. Perhaps I misjudged him.

I sit on a wooden seat just across from the grave and let the sun soak my face and I think about being a young man again, about impetuosity and ideals and possibilities and the careless craziness of uncontaminated faith. And I think about the relative comfort – or numbness – of middle age. And then I think about the old man whose body is buried six feet under this dry, red clay. And about what he said that night on the back step of the bar.

'I can't work with the earth anymore.'

'That's okay,' I told him. 'There's always food here. Always. You know that. You'll never go short as long as I'm here.'

He was silent for a while, holding his sandwich, not eating.

'The earth is not just about food,' he said eventually, quietly and coherently. 'It's about where we come from, who we are and where we're going. All my life I've had my hands in it, had it under my nails, felt the way it stings your arms in the evening after you've spent the day working it. I've never been away from the earth and I knew, from the time I was a young man, that whenever I couldn't work it, it would take me back.'

'Really?'

'Yes. That's what they mean when they say earth to earth. Whoever wrote those words knew what he was talking about; he was a countryman or at least a man who knew the soil.'

'That's good to know,' I said because I couldn't think of anything else to say.

And then the old man had gone back to eating his sandwich and I'd pulled on my cigarette and whistled the cobalt smoke out in rings, into the fading summer light.

'Am I talking too much?' he asked after a while.

'Not at all.'

'You don't talk a lot.'

'I talk all the time when I'm inside,' I beckoned through the open doorway, to the bar behind me.

'That's just yap,' he said.

'Yes.'

'Beyond that?'

'No, not a lot.'

'The times in our lives when we say too much are the ones that really count, the times when we step across the borderline between who people think we are and who we truly know ourselves to be.'

I didn't answer, didn't come out with some platitude.

'I know some of what happened,' the old man said. 'I don't know all of it but whatever it was is said and done and over. If you crossed some boundary back then, so be it. I have no doubt you did it for what you thought were the right reasons.'

'How did you know about all this?'

'I know a lot less, probably, than there is to know.'

'But some things – you obviously know some things.' I flicked my cigarette nervously across the yard and it flared in the warm breeze and then faded slowly.

'Like you, I didn't always live here,' the old man said. 'I went places, saw things, heard stories, I even got to listen to him once.'

I nodded.

He went back to eating his sandwich.

'There was a lot of stuff,' I said. 'In the end. A lot of weird stuff.'

I saw his head move up and down in the falling darkness.

'Not him. Us. We were all fucked up, frightened, more than frightened, terrified for ourselves. And disappointed. It didn't end the way we hoped it would.'

'Most things don't.'

'And now I listen to this guy on the TV, trying to turn it all into something it was never meant to be. I read him in the papers. He wasn't there. He doesn't know the truth. He has bits of the story; he adds bits, he spins it.'

'Always happens,' the old man said. 'Someone does something good and moves on, someone else makes a career out of picking over the pieces. Anyway, that's not my concern. Or yours. You hold on to the truth. The truth will set you free.'

'Not in my experience,' I said bitterly. 'All it'll do is hand someone an excuse to give you a good kicking. Last time I told the truth I got my marching orders.'

'The voice of experience,' the old man laughed and then pushed himself up slowly, one hand on the step and one on my shoulder.

'Anyway,' he said again. 'Anyway....'

I stood up too and waited for him to steady himself.

'Thank you for the food,' he said. 'I hope I didn't seem ungrateful.'

'You're welcome. Any time. You know that. Any time.'

He began to move across the yard, then stopped and turned. I could see his face in the light from the kitchen door.

'As long as you do it to the least of my comrades. Wasn't that it?'

'That was it,' I said.

'He was a good man.'

'He was.'

'It was a good thought.'

'It was.'

'Get back to the land, when you can,' he said. 'They can't kill all the unbelievers.'

I nodded and then he turned and slipped away into the darkness of the lane outside.

That was a couple of months before he died. In the meantime, he came and went. Sometimes I'd see him every day for a week and sometimes I wouldn't see him for five or six days. When it got to the eighth day without his calling, I reported it to the police. They found him, or what was left of him, the following week.

I go on sitting on the wooden seat, watching the cracks of light between the lines of staggered headstones, catching a glimpse of a mound of vanishing colour on a fresh grave here, a vase or an urn with plastic blossoms there, and everywhere the tinted stones, the short grass, the neat kerbs about the graves.

Is this really getting back to the earth, I wonder? Can the old man possibly be at rest here? I come to the conclusion that he can't. Whatever earth there was in this field is hidden now, closed, cemented, divided into plots of glimmering stones or scraps of greenery, for fear the sight of the red clay might remind the passers-by that death is not some homogenised and pretty sleeping place, that it's not the same as life, though we sometimes try to pretend it is.

It's quite possible that Henry would have preferred the rats to have finished the job, leaving only his bones to the rain, and they in time would have melted slowly back into the ground from which he'd drawn his sustenance. I'll never really know but I've done what I've done and I can only hope he somehow understands that it was done for the best of reasons.

My eye travels over the stone again. His name, his dates, and at the bottom the only words I could think of when they asked me what I wanted written.

Go Home to Your Friends

The first time I saw Jude was on a hot day at the end of May. He was walking in the shadows between two buildings. I wish I'd had my camera with me then, to have caught that first sight of the tall young man I was to love, still love, for ever. But let me begin with a photograph. It may look ordinary to you, another photograph of a still, pale room looking out over the ocean. The curtains are drawn back on the ceiling-high double window that opens onto a sun-scalded balcony. There's a low, wide bed on which the sheets are tightly stretched. Across the room, against the whitewashed wall, is a sea-blue chest. A Shaker simple room.

Outside the open window, on the balcony, is a high wooden chair.

The photograph is black and white, of course. It gives you a feel for the room, for the beauty of its plainness. It tells you a lot, but it doesn't tell you everything. There are things here that you cannot see, things out of sight of the camera, and, off this room, there are other rooms, which make up the apartment that is my home.

This photograph is like those books they've written about the Captain. It tells you things but not everything. You look at it and you see the bed, the chest, the curtains, the windows and the edge of the chair on the balcony. But, no matter how long you look or how hard you try to see beyond the haze that is the world outside the open windows, you can't. You can dredge up baskets of memory and experience, empty out the pieces that will make your own picture but it'll be nothing more than imagination. Feel free to use my photograph, to rearrange the furniture, to have the breeze lift and drape and shape and reshape the curtains. Feel free to close the windows on the summer wind.

Ahnehmoss. Ahnehmoss. I repeat the word, but quietly because I am still embarrassed that I'll mispronounce the wind that's lifting the curtains at the other side of the room. The first time I heard that word spoken was on the bank of the brown river where Jude and I lay, destined but uncertain. My hands were behind my head because I couldn't trust myself to leave them free and so I kept them cupped between my hair and the earth and the sun was strong and the wind blew and bloated our shirts and he said ahnehmoss.

He was learning Greek then. Not content with medical studies and politics, he had to have another language, too. He talked about Greece all the time. He was Che and Greece was his Bolivia. Greek history, ancient and modern, the people, the culture, the heroes and the language, were constants in his life. I admired his passion and his energy. Whatever he believed, he pursued with a fire and I was happy to be the object of that ardour. I don't know if I supposed I'd ever be the most important thing in Jude's life. I don't think the question ever raised itself in my head. I was too happy being with him, too keyed-up with expectation. Looking back from this distance, it's impossible to describe the intensity that was between us. When I say I lay with my hands behind my head to keep myself from touching him, I mean just that. I wanted to touch him all the time, I wanted my tongue in his mouth all the time, I wanted him to love me all the time, to make love to me. Whatever he wanted, I was willing to give. I have never loved anyone before or since. Life and art and sex melt before the remembrance of that love. I learned many things from those days with Jude – that love existed for me and that I will never reach such gracious and blazing depths again. That it was a time of madness and losing it drove me mad for a time.

Writing about those days is hopeless because I can't tell you anything that will make any sense. Reason and intellect had nothing to do with that part of our lives. And memory is a useless device when it comes to redeeming passion. Those days and the people we were then are beyond redemption anyway. That's something I've learned in the years since. Sometimes, when I don't stop myself in time and I drift back to youth and eagerness and excitement, when I'm touched by madness again, I sense the pain and, beyond it, the exhilaration and the tightness, the sensuality. It can never be recovered but it never quite disappears. I remind myself, then, that true love does exist, that it's not just the acceptance of the best you can get. Anyone who tells you that is lying.

But trying to describe this to you, if you've never been burned or maddened or despaired, is a hopeless task. All I can do is give the facts, show the photographs, repeat the version I remember. The real story has burned a hole in my heart and I have neither the words nor the strength to tell it. Sometimes it comes like a thundercloud and the day is plunged into desperation. And sometimes it whips everything from the atmosphere and I can barely breathe. The air is expectant. I wait for his face at the window, the outline of his body on the balcony. I close my eyes and expect the weight of his body on my bed, my fingers become his fingers inside me, my hand is his hand on the back of my head.

Sometimes I think I could have been like him. In some ways I am. Let me tell you a story. Years ago, long after Jude and I were separated, I was walking down a street in London. I was coming back from covering some protest or other. It was a hot summer evening and I wasn't in any particular hurry. There hadn't been any bloodshed and I knew my photos weren't going to make the front page or any page. I had my cameras over my shoulder and I was cutting through an alley when an old man, sitting on a plastic crate at the side of a skip, asked me for some money. I stopped and took some change from my jeans and then I asked him if I could take his photograph.

'If you want,' he said.

So I took a few shots and, while I did, we chatted. It was nothing much, no great, deep conversation. When I'd finished, I began packing my camera.

'It's good for me to talk to decent people,' the old man said. 'It was part of my life at one time. I know it's the old cliché but I had the house, the beautiful wife – she was beautiful. Things like that don't ever leave your mind, just because you've lost them.'

'I know.'

'You're beautiful,' he said and I thought his voice was going to break.

I put my camera bag on the ground and hunkered down in front of him. I lifted my T-shirt, took his hand and put it on my breast. His fingers were surprisingly soft on my skin. I thought I was being kind. I was trying to be kind. I was thinking of Jude as I did it, thinking about giving, that's all that was in my head. But the old man took his hand away, gently but quickly.

'You can't undo what I did.'

I wasn't embarrassed by his words. I imagined Jude looking disapprovingly at me. Telling me I had strange notions of generosity.

'I didn't mean to offend you,' I said.

The old man smiled.

'I'm not offended.'

Walking away, along the crowded teatime streets, back in the office, I was pleased that I hadn't thought twice. It made me happy that I'd done something unsafe.

It's not all gone yet, I thought, standing in the darkroom, giggling. There was no rush of elation, just a quiet satisfaction that I hadn't become entirely predictable. I'd done something that would have been typical of me twenty years earlier, something that refreshed me and proved that the other, younger me was still alive.

Sometimes that kind of thing, my spur of the moment generosity, annoyed Jude.

'You confuse licence with assistance,' he'd say.

'And you think the only offering that counts is the political.'

'Physical beauty is no cure for poverty.'

'It depends on the poverty.'

And so the gentle arguments would go. And I can hear him now, hear what he'd say.

'Showing your tits won't change the world; you can't believe it will.'

'If you think that's all there is to it,' I'd say, 'you don't understand anything about the moments that alter people's lives.'

In spite of everything, in spite of his beauty and his own sensuousness and his burning sexuality, Jude had a very proper streak. For me it was different. I didn't go to bed with people or fuck them without thinking but, sometimes I saw my body, and whatever beauty it possessed, as something that was capable of bringing comfort to someone in need.

And I never had sex with anyone else while Jude and I were together. He knew that but it suited him, at times, to pretend otherwise. It gave him reasons to be angry when his anger should have been directed elsewhere. And, though he'd deny this, it probably added to his passion for me. Men can be like that: they covet what they claim to despise.

I hated having to justify myself, feeling that there was a need for some kind of excuse for any generosity I felt.

I know, in the years since then, that among his friends I've become some kind of mythological woman with an insatiable sexual appetite. I've read the stories, veiled and half-veiled, the rumours and accusations. They're all there, in books and newspapers and magazines. Sometimes I'm supposed to be two or three different women, at times I'm one. Occasionally I have a name but it's never my own name; they never get that right. That sexual predator never appears as Lily. Mary has become a favourite; it's common enough to be safe and it sets up this confusion, adds a little more spice to the mixture.

They have no idea about the reality, even the ones who claim to have researched the story. They start from the same points of ignorance and misinformation, assuming that I was a whore who'd slept with the Captain or tried to sleep with him. Or, sometimes, the women don't feature at all. It's all whittled down to a clash of ideologies, between Jude and the ones who played follow-the-leader. That really gets to me. That's why I wanted to go back. I felt I owed it to Jude. I wanted to talk to the people the reporters never talk to, to let those people tell their stories. I wanted the truth.

But, most of all, I wanted to hear my own story, to find out why the things that happened to me were done. To put faces on those who did them.

Ahnehmoss

The warm wind lifts the curtains and I sit here and watch them fold and fall, again. I think of the rain in London, the torrential, cold and shearing rain that fell in wintertime. I think of the queues for taxis, the stale smell of soaking clothes, the dampness in my flat, drab wool unravelling across the sky to blanket out the sun.

I thought, when I moved back there, that it was the great escape. No incessant heat, no blue skies to remind me, no hard and angled shadows from the whitewashed buildings, no bright, raucous colours on the windows and doors of houses. London was drab, and drabness was what I needed. I'd had enough of intensity and brilliance and enough of the confusion that, for eight months, passed for life. I needed to be a no one in a nowhere world. I needed to get back to the consolation of the banal. Saturday afternoons photographing football matches at Stamford Bridge, Saturday nights catching someone's arrival at the Albert Hall, children on swings, old men in alleyways, even lottery millionaires in the spray of champagne. Their fame was unimportant. My anonymity was everything. I could begin to recover my reason in all that. Nothing much was happening and that was enough for me.

But, much and all as I needed to go back to London, to see and feel the greyness that bound my wounds like spiders' webs, I could not go back to Dublin. I was afraid of the places that were Jude's and mine. Afraid of the memories I'd meet on night-time streets and even more of the ghosts who might appear in the sunny places between the rain.

But I'm not afraid anymore. I'm not afraid of anything. And I've come back to this once familiar place, this place that once, briefly, was home. I can live here now. I can face the sunshine and the blue skies and the singing walls and humming doors. I'm not afraid of the light or the past.

You can rearrange the furniture in my photographs, you can dredge up the versions of memory that suit your own point of view. I don't care. I've tried to live in spite of the past and now I can live with it. I'm happy here with the wind coming in off the flat blue sea.

The first time I saw Jude was on a hot day at the end of May. He was walking in the shadows between two buildings. I was twenty-three years old then and he was twenty-two. I was in my final year in art college, studying photography, and he was in medical school. I thought he was beautiful. I wished I had my camera with me but I didn't. So, instead, I stopped him and asked if I could photograph him later. He laughed out loud and blushed.

'Who put you up to this?'

'Eros,' I said.

His mouth was a crooked grin.

'And me,' I added.

'And why do you want to photograph me?'

'Because you're beautiful.'

He blushed again.

'Well, I have an anatomy exam tomorrow. And another exam on Friday, so if you think my beauty will keep til the weekend….'

'It'll keep.'

'It doesn't always,' he said and his face was serious. 'I've seen bodies go off in twenty-four hours.'

'I'll take my chances.'

'Well,' he said and he was grinning again. 'The best planned lays of mice and men….'

'I just want to photograph you.'

'I was joking. I've been waiting two weeks to use that line.'

We exchanged phone numbers and then I kissed him.

'Rejoice, rejoice, you have no choice,' he said, when I'd finished.

I wanted to ask if he was as good at making love as he was at smart-assing, but I didn't.

And that was it.

We met on the following Saturday. By then, I'd already, secretly, taken two rolls of him, walking in Grafton Street, in Stephen's Green, on Baggot Street. I couldn't wait. I followed him to and from his exams and found out where he lived. I made a game of it but it wasn't a game. I was besotted with him but I knew I might frighten him, so, when we met and I'd taken my photographs, we went walking in the sunshine and lay by the brown river and I kept my hands behind my head.

That image returns. Often. Two figures on the riverbank, hands behind their heads, the willow branches bending above them and, up the hill, a red chestnut fanning out over the long grass.

Us.

I've tried to capture that moment all over the world, lovers lying by water, not touching, lovers at country streams, lovers by the seashore. But I know the task is hopeless. I've never found another woman whose body aches out loud; whose skin is so tight with anticipation; whose hands are clenched uncomfortably beneath the nape of her neck. I've never found me.

For two weeks I went with Jude to places where I wanted to photograph him but I never touched him. I kept myself to myself. I knew he was waiting for another kiss, like the first kiss but harder.

He called me the Maid of As'tolat, because she died with a lily in her hand, and I called him Jude the Demure, because it annoyed him.

In the end, he asked me to stay with him and I did and I always will.

They theorise about everything, the researchers and journalists and writers and quick-buck merchants. About the Captain's politics, about Jude's politics, about Jude and me and the Captain and me, about betrayal, ambition, money, disillusion, ritual and consequence. As if any of those things were important.

They miss the point that we were living our lives. We weren't standing outside those lives analysing everything; we were right in the middle of them, alive, laughing, making mistakes. We were sleeping and breathing and earning a living, getting on with things, we were doing the best we could in circumstances that were sometimes dangerous but often predictable and ordinary.

I have never once read anything that mentioned the laughter or the music or the abandoned fun that were regular parts of our lives. I've never seen a picture that showed the Captain smiling. It's as though no one believes he ever smiled. I could show you pictures of him sitting on a raft, his face illuminated with laughter. Or one of him standing near the back of some house, his hands angled to catch the sun, making shadow pictures of a donkey and a duck on the rough stone wall. Or one of him singing, his eyes closed, a smile on his lips, lost in the music. I've never read about how fine a singer he was, never heard anyone mention it.

The first time I heard the Captain sing, the music felt like it had hurt me. It was late one night and I was making coffee in the kitchen of the old house he shared with some of the others near the beach. Gradually I became aware of this voice in the air, not loud, not demanding, not wanting attention, just there. I couldn't even hear the guitar behind it. I'd never heard the Captain sing and I'd never heard the song, but I stopped to listen, catching a couple of lines.

Let your love cover me,
like a pair of angel wings,
you are my family,
you are my family.

I followed the voice, down the short corridor to the open door of his room. He was sitting on his low bed, his back to the door, singing and playing. And then, sensing me behind him, he stopped and turned.

'Is that your song?' I asked.

He shook his head and smiled.

'I wish. It's a Pierce Pettis song.'

'Don't know his music,' I said.

'You should.'

'You sing it well.'

'Not as well as he does.'

'Can I hear the rest of it?'

'Sure, but you don't have to stand in the doorway.'

I smiled and stepped into his room.

'Chair,' he nodded.

I sat.

'What's the betting I make a mess of it this time? An audience of one – is that an audient?'

I smiled.

'Right,' he took a deep breath but seemed uneasy at the prospect of singing for me.

'You don't have to,' I said quietly.

'No, I do, I do. There are a lot of things that appear easy but aren't.'

'For you?'

'Yes.'

'But you do them.'

'Yes.'

'Why?'

He shrugged and paused.

'Probably for the same reason Jude does what he does. The same reason you take your photographs. The same reason people go to work in dead-end jobs. Needing to, having to.... Can I sing the song now?' he smiled.

'Sure,' I said. 'Sure. I'm sorry. You must be sick of people asking you these things.'

Crossing his eyes, he stuck his tongue out and mimicked a vomit. I laughed.

'The song!' he said and began to pick the strings of his guitar and then to sing very quietly, his voice clear and steady.

Can you fix this? It's a broken heart,
it was fine but it just fell apart.
It was mine but now I give it to you,
cause you can fix it, you know what to do.

No one ever wrote the truth about Jude. No one bothered with the fact that they were both men, just men, doing their best. Why do dreams and aspirations bring the expectation of perfection? Isn't it typical of people to think that a dream not coming true makes the dream a mistake and the dreamer a failure? It's as though disappointment makes something worthless or, worse still, a crime. The truth is each of us was flawed. That's what made us the people we were.

The man I knew was angry and had an appetite for justice. But he was beautiful, too, and gentle and driven. He couldn't be what I wanted him to be, just as he couldn't be what the Captain wanted him to be either. Jude was never comfortable in his own skin; it took me a little time to recognise that but I'm not sure that the Captain ever did. So how could we expect him to be comfortable with other people's expectations?

People talk about Jude as though he had this enormous ego. He didn't. When I first asked to photograph him and told him he was beautiful, he was genuinely unsettled. And when he talked about bodies going off, he was serious. He put no store by the attraction of the body or the beauty of art or the charm of words.

Once or twice I watched Jude while he listened to the Captain speak, holding the crowds enthralled. Jude's mind was clearly elsewhere, planning, considering the options. Had he still been around, things would never have ended as they did and, certainly, the things that happened after the Captain's death would never have happened. But, given the people who were left with the Captain, there was an inevitability about those events. Just as there was an inevitability about the fact that Jude wouldn't and couldn't be involved in all the politicking and posturing that went on.

Jude's decision had nothing to do with the Captain, nor had it anything to do with me. I can imagine some small-time journalist picking up on the story of that night when I first heard the Captain singing and turning it into a low-life pitch at pornography, getting us into bed in five sentences, laying the blame for Jude's leaving at my feet. They've done it already, so I suppose it doesn't matter anyway. I can't fall any further in their estimation, nor they in mine. I don't blame the Captain for Jude's going and I don't blame Jude for leaving. In the weeks after he went, I was distraught, not because I cared about the Captain's future or what might or might not happen to his companions but because I missed Jude.

I didn't fall in love with his politics, I fell in love with him – his passion, his anger, his beauty, his sexuality, his body, his smile, the way he made love to me, the way he wanted me to make love to him. Those who write him off as a traitor know nothing of him. They just read each other's headlines.

He told me he was going. He didn't tell me where and I didn't ask. I hoped he might ask me to go with him, although I never expected that offer. The night before he left, we sat on a swing in the garden. A light, warm rain was falling and the wooden overhang was sheltering us. I sensed what he was about to say but many times in the previous weeks I had expected him to say something about going and he hadn't.

It was obvious that he had no patience with how things were progressing – or not progressing, as he saw it. He believed the Captain was following a middle ground that was neither wholly political nor wholly committed to revolution.

'All we're doing is hanging our flags out for them to come and get us,' Jude had said a couple of days earlier. 'If you want to be a politician, be a politician. But you can't be all things to everyone. You can't preach peace and hope for change; it just plays into their hands. And the fact is the political road has been closed for a long time now. Closed and dug up. Not only is it not going anywhere, it's not even an option anymore.'

The Captain listened. They all listened, but I don't think the others ever truly trusted Jude. They imagined him to have a superiority complex when in fact he was simply frustrated by their lack of organisation and ambition.

That evening, he and the Captain had sat in the bedroom for a long time, the door closed, Jude's voice coming in waves, the Captain's voice barely discernible. I was in bed when Jude came into our room.

'I don't want to talk about any of this stuff,' he said, before I could ask anything. 'I just want you to fuck me.'

And that's how it was, then and in the nights that followed. Nights of intense sex followed by days of silent brooding. So, when that warm, rainy evening came and Jude told me he was going, I wasn't surprised.

'Have you decided where?' I asked.

'Yes, but what you don't know can't lead you into trouble.'

'Will I hear from you again?'

'Of course.'

'Will I see you again, be with you again.'

He nodded.

'But you don't want me to go with you?'

'No. Not this time. I don't think you should stay here either.'

'Why?'

'Things will change soon, very soon, for the worse. Best you go somewhere else, London or Dublin, anywhere that's away from here. I'll write to you when I get where I'm going.'

'And that's it?'

'No, that's not it. That's just the end of this part of things; it's not the end of us, you know that, Lily. You know that.'

I did but I was frightened.

'What if something happens?'

'Something always happens; things happen all the time. Sometimes the things that seem safest are the most dangerous things.'

'So when are you going?'

'Tomorrow. I need a day's head start. I don't trust them. I need you to cover for me, to say I have an extra shift at the hospital tomorrow night.'

'All right,' I said. 'This is devastating.'

'Yes,' Jude nodded. 'But it won't always be.'

We made love that night and he came inside me, twice. I hoped I was pregnant but I wasn't. Two days later the Captain found me and sat with me in the garden.

'He's gone,' he said.

'Yes.'

'We both knew he would leave.'

'Yes.'

'You're welcome to stay or go. You know that.'

'Thank you.'

'I'm sorry he left.'

'I know.'

'We talked. He probably told you.'

'No,' I said. 'He didn't tell me anything about the conversation.'

He nodded slowly and smiled.

'He's a passionate man,' I said.

'I know that. I hope you two will be happy together in the future.'

'I hope so.'

I heard from Jude once, five days after he'd left, a short telephone call at a time when he knew the house would be quiet. He was safe and in good spirits. He was leaving the country that night; he and three other men had arranged for a boat to take them across the straits. He'd be in touch soon. He loved me. He asked me to wish the Captain well.

There were conflicting stories. A motorboat with the five men in it had hit rough seas and capsized. It had been rammed accidentally, in heavy fog, by a freighter. It had been blown out of the water by a patrol boat. The TV reports and the newspapers said a bomb on board had detonated accidentally, that the men were terrorists and had been planning to blow up the presidential yacht. Four bodies were recovered, Jude's among them. They were buried in a cemetery near the ocean. I have never visited the place. I never will.

The Captain rang me when the news reached him. I was visiting a friend on the other side of the city.

'You should go,' he said.

'I will.'

'You should go now. This will bring them down on us.'

'Why?'

'They'll use it. They'll link us to Jude and use it to corner us.'

'That's not what he intended.'

'I know that but it won't matter.'

There was a moment's silence between us.

'If we don't meet again, thank you for the photographs and the friendship and for being with us.'

'I'm glad we met,' I said.

'Me too.'

And then the line went dead.

I read about the Captain's death five weeks afterwards. I was in Barcelona. Later, much later, at the end of that year, the other rumours began to trickle out but I paid them scant attention. I had no faith in the tellers of the stories and, to be truthful, I had little interest in him. The Captain's death brought a sadness. Jude's brought a wretchedness that lasted for years and hasn't, in truth, ever gone away, nor ever will.

In the past few weeks, I've been thinking about photographs as much as taking them. A publisher approached me about putting together a collection to make a book. I was flattered until I realised what he was doing. He was looking for photographs of the Captain, or even just one unpublished image that would be a hinge on which to hang publicity for the book. So I said no. But it set me thinking and looking, back through twenty-five years of work. And it got me thinking even more about Jude, not that there's been a single day, since that hot afternoon in the long ago summer, when I've not thought about him.

Jude was passionate about the things he did and it was that passion that drove him through his life and brought him to the Captain's side and then away again. And it was that passion that led him to the place where it all ended.

My work didn't interest him enough to make him passionate. He rarely asked me about it, rarely made suggestions or criticisms, never praised it or questioned it or analysed it. I presume he thought it was flippant, middle-class, superfluous. Only once did he ever refer directly to what I did. It was in the months before he and the Captain were killed.

We had come out of a meeting and were passing a graveyard. I stopped to watch two men filling in a grave. The way they worked, the rhythm of their shovelling had a loveliness and a grace that was like music.

'I wish there was a way to capture that on film,' I said.

'Movies,' Jude said.

'I meant in a photograph.'

He nodded. We walked on a few yards and then he stopped and put his hands on my shoulders and looked into my eyes.

'I do know what you mean,' he said. 'I do. When I sat behind you at the meeting this morning, I wished I'd had a camera, to photograph the nape of your neck, to freeze that one image. The way you have your hair tied up, that little hollow there.'

He put a finger on the back of my neck, tracing the dip on my skin.

'To be able to take one perfect photograph of your neck, something I could look at and touch or not touch, just dream of touching.'

And then he blushed and smiled and put his arm around me and held me for a moment.

So, these evenings, when the hot sun is sliding down the sky beyond my balcony, I set up the camera and try to make that photograph. I sit with my back to the world and click the timer button again and again and again. I want this image to be as good as I can make it. I want the wisps of my hair to be like summer straw. I want the shadows to fall like lovers, intertwined.

Sacred Heart

He sits in his car. It's late in the afternoon and the last of the autumn light is being wrung from the heavens, dribbling down onto the flaky, rusted stubble of a long, wide field. He watches an old crow flail jadedly across the dull September sky, in search of its rookery, and he thinks of his young daughter running carelessly along the beach, her sun-bleached hair flying like a thousand short kite strings.

And he remembers the shadow of a gull on the warm summer sand.

'Look,' his daughter says. 'Look, there's a bird under the sand.'

'That's a sand gull,' he says.

'What's a sand gull?'

'It's a magic bird. It can fly on the sand or under the sand. You can see it but if you try to touch it, it isn't there.'

She looks at him quizzically.

'See,' he says, pointing to the circling shadow.

His daughter watches the silhouette darken and lighten as the bird swoops and rises unseen above her head.

'What does he eat?' she asks.

'He eats the wind.'

'Does he?'

'Yes.'

'Why don't we see him every day?'

'Because he only appears to children who are very good and even then just once in a blue moon.'

She throws him that look again.

'The moon's not blue.'

'Sometimes it is.'

'I never saw it blue.'

'Do you remember the first night we were in America?'

'Yes.'

'Do you remember the moon when we came out of the airport building?'

'Yes.'

'Do you remember what colour it was?'

'Orange.'

'See. You'd never seen an orange moon before that but there it was. And you've never seen blue moon but you will.'

'Tonight?'

He shrugged. 'You never know. It'll be there when you least expect it and when you most need it.'

'What does that mean?'

'You're full of questions.' He laughs, swinging his daughter high into the air, twirling her above the sand and sea, throwing her into the sunny sky and catching her as she falls in a shower of laughter.

And out of nowhere, as it always comes, the memory. He is dancing with his wife, her head against his chest, her body warm against his own, her hands light on his shoulders, his arms around her waist, the music moving them in some slowed-down version of a waltz, and he shivers in the burning sun and looks at his daughter and he feels a desperate, surging need to know that she will have happiness in her life.

'The sand gull is gone,' the little girl says.

'It'll be back.'

'Will it?'

'Of course. It always comes back to good girls. Always.'

She smiles and he hugs her and puts her back down in the warm shallows of the Atlantic water.

'You know the way you write in your little book every night?'

He nods.

'Why do you do that?'

'I'm keeping a diary of our holiday.'

'Why?'

'Because it's special – just you and me.'

'Are you keeping it to read to Mum when we get home?'

'No, but I could.'

'What does it say?'

'Lots of things.'

'Like?'

'Like about what we do each day, about the sea and the weather and where we've been and things I've been thinking, and tonight I'll write about the sand gull.'

'Will you read it to me tonight?'

'Okay.'

'Will you read it to me every night?'

'Yes, okay.'

'Promise?'

'Promise.'

They paddle on, the sunlight surging over them like a reassurance.

'Don't forget to look for the sand dollars,' he says and they lower their heads and walk slowly, eyes scanning the shining sand.

That night, as he tucks his daughter into bed in her air-conditioned room, she reminds him of his promise to read from his diary.

'I haven't written today's entry yet.'

'Well read me something.'

'It'll be boring.'

'I'll tell you if I'm bored.'

He goes into his room and returns with a notebook.

'Is that your diary?'

'Yes.'

She settles herself against the soft pillow and waits.

'This is from the first day.'

She nods. He clears his throat.

'"The heat when we came out of the airport building was like a wall. We'd been warned but I wasn't expecting it."'

'That's silly, it wasn't a wall,' his daughter says. 'It was just hot. If it was a wall, we wouldn't have been able to get out, unless it fell, and if it fell it might have squished us.'

'Told you it'd bore you.'

'Read more. I'll see.'

'"I like the way the houses here are built into the woods. When they build, they use the landscape; they don't clear everything. They knock as few trees as possible and then they put up the timber frames and block-build around them. As we drove down from the airport, coming through the tobacco fields, the skies opened and we had a glorious thunderstorm."'

He pauses.

'That's okay. I kind of like that. Read me something about the beach. About us at the beach.'

He leafs through the pages of the notebook

'Okay, here's something, but you may not understand it. "There are several houses strung along the beach, straight out of *Summer of '42*." That's a film, there were houses in it like the houses along the beach.'

'I think I know what you mean. You don't have to explain everything. I'll stop you if I want to ask you something.'

'Yes, Miss.'

'Now go on.'

'"The heat on the beach is intense but the breeze makes it manageable. I've been careful that L doesn't get burned."'

'L. That's me. Why didn't you write Lynn?'

'I was writing fast. I was tired.'

'Oh, okay. Go on then.'

'"The only things that are annoying on the beach are the jets from the airfield down the coast. They come in loud and low and really should be farther out to sea."'

He notices her nod gravely.

'It's just that kind of stuff.'

'Well, why don't you write more interesting things, like about the sand gulls and the sand dollars and stuff. You can write them before I go to bed and then read them to me and I'll tell you what I think.'

'That sounds like a very good idea.'

'Now,' his daughter says. 'I'm tired.'

She reaches up, wraps her hands around his neck and kisses his cheek.

'Goodnight, Daddy.'

'Goodnight, sweetheart. I love you.'

'I love you.'

She turns, nesting her head in the pillow, closes her eyes and smiles.

In the morning they go body-boarding in the shallows but his daughter is terrified by the sound of the breaking waves and he takes her back to the swimming pool near the apartment and that night writes his diary entry while she's in the bath and reads it to her as he tucks her in.

'"I miss trees here – deciduous trees. The sea is pleasant when it's warm but it's too changeable. Trees change, too, but differently, more slowly. And they have the sound of the sea in their leaves. The sea is not so constant, regular yes but capable of great unpredictability and viciousness and the power to swallow. In the forest the change is more gradual, leaves fall, trees fall but there's a peacefulness and a smell of growth, not threat. And saplings, leaves unfolding, flowers, even the smell of cut wood.""

'I'm sorry that you miss the trees,' his daughter says.

'That's okay. I'll get back to them.'

'And I miss Mum sometimes.'

'That's good, too, and you'll get back to her soon.'

Later, he sits in the tarn of light from the reading lamp. Outside, beyond his glassed reflection, the sky flares and fades with distant lightning above the rumbling sea. He turns a page of *Lifting the Latch* and reads of Stow and Adlestrop and Oxford. The names are freshly beautiful in the American heat. He remembers them as villages and cities emerging from the English summer haze and he catches his own slight smile in the mirroring glass.

His daughter is playing in the shallows of the sea. Another young girl, more or less her own age, is playing with her. Together they build a sand dam and giggle as the surging ripples eat the walls away so that they can start again, a foot closer to the high watermark.

He stands with the girl's father.

'You'd think they've known each other for ever,' the man says.

'Yes.'

'I'm Ken, by the way.'

'Al,' he says and proffers a hand.

'Vacationing?'

'Yes. For three weeks.'

'Couldn't have chosen a more remarkably picturesque place.'

'No.'

'Been coming here since I was a kid myself.'

'You're lucky.'

'Yeah, I guess I am, blessed with the good fortune of being born in the land of the true and the home of the brave and the beautiful.'

The girls move again, hunkering in the warm, slow water.

'By the way,' the man says. 'My daughter's first name is Melissa.'

'And this is Lynn.'

'You're European?'

'Yes.'

'English?'

'Irish.'

Ken nods and smiles.

'Always appreciated here.'

'Thank you.'

They stand together, watching the children play.

He watches his daughter building sand castles in the rising morning heat. He lifts a piece of driftwood from the beach and carries it to her.

'Sand only.' She waves him away.

He smiles and runs his fingers along the bleached and faded timber. He thinks about how the sea wears everything to a smoothness – shells, stones, timber, wire and glass. How, by the time they wash up here, every jagged rim has been robbed of its roughness and its edge.

'Homogenised,' he says out loud but his daughter appears not to hear him.

Back in the apartment, making sandwiches for their lunch, he turns on the radio. Judy Collins is singing 'Jerusalem'. He stands transfixed while Blake's words pour over him.

And did those feet in ancient time
Walk upon England's mountains green?

And was the holy Lamb of God
On England's pleasant pastures seen?

And did the Countenance Divine
Shine forth upon our clouded hills?
And was Jerusalem builded here
Among these dark Satanic Mills?

Bring me my bow of burning gold!
Bring me my arrows of desire!
Bring me my spear! O clouds, unfold!
Bring me my chariot of fire!

I will not cease from mental fight,
Nor shall my sword sleep in my hand,
Till we have built Jerusalem
In England's green and pleasant land.

Later, at that time where day and night begin to merge, he walks with his daughter on the orange sand and they find a long scarf of seaweed.

'What's that?' his daughter asks.

'It's a small sea dragon,' he says, lifting the golden green ridges in his hands.

His daughter looks at him, searching for a give-away twist of the mouth but, finding none, she returns her gaze to the puckered shape that rests against her father's arm.

'It's sleeping,' he says quietly.

'Can it make fire?'

'Not the sea dragon. Fire and water don't mix. Do you want to touch it?'

The girl is uncertain.

'It won't bite,' he says.

She lays an uneasy hand against the slippery seaweed.

'It's soft.'

'Yes.'

'And it won't bite me?'

'No.'

Again, she touches the spongy, wet crests.

'Would you like to put it back into the sea? That's where it belongs.'

'All right.'

Gently he drapes the ribbon of seaweed across her palms and she carries it down to the murky sea and lays it delicately in the small waves. Together they watch it blend into the dark water, retreating with the receding waves until it disappears into the wide Atlantic.

'You're a lucky girl.'

'Why?'

'You've seen a sand gull and a sea dragon. Some people live their whole lives and never see either.'

'Do they?'

'Yes, they do,' he says and realises the night has fallen. 'Time for us to head for home.'

'Will we be able to find home?' the girl asks, suddenly aware of the darkness.

'We'll follow the lights.'

Feeling the sand crabs scuttle across his feet, he swings his daughter onto his shoulder, turns his back on the black, uncertain water and moves towards the lighted windows.

He is sitting at the table, writing about the sand crabs, when the telephone rings.

He considers not answering but he knows it will ring and ring, every two or three minutes until he does.

'Hello.'

'Hello. Al?' His wife's voice from halfway across the world.

'How are you?'

'Fine. How's Lynn?'

'She's really well. She's sleeping.'

'At this hour? Is she sick?'

'It's midnight here.'

'Oh right, of course.'

Silence spans the thousands of miles.

'When will you bring her back?'

'Sorry?'

'When will you bring Lynn back to me?'

'Why are you asking this? You know when we're back,' he says quietly, forcing himself to be calm.

'I know nothing. Who's there with you?'

'Lynn. She's sleeping, like I said.'

'Why are you whispering? There's someone in the apartment, isn't there?'

'There is no one else here. I was sitting alone writing my diary. Lynn is sleeping.'

'Put her on to me.'

'She's asleep.'

'There's someone else there.'

'There is no one else here, just the pair of us, as you and I agreed, Lynn and me, for three weeks. That's it. No one else.'

'I don't believe you.'

'It's the truth.'

'Are you feeding her properly?'

'Yes. She's eating really well. Lots of fresh air, lots of good food, lots of sleep.'

'And you're putting her suncream on?'

'Yes.'

'Factor fifty.'

'Yes.'

Another silence and he imagines the waves rolling over the buried telephone cables.

'You realise how much the legal fees are going to be?' she asks.

'I'll pay them. All of them.'

'You realise this is an act of gross selfishness?'

'Yes.'

'And I don't believe there's no one else there. I don't believe there isn't someone else.'

He scratches his forehead and sighs very quietly.

'We'll talk about it when Lynn and I get home. Back,' he corrects himself. 'I'll have Lynn ring you in the morning at eight, that'll be one in the afternoon your time.'

'Will you?'

'Yes, of course.'

'And there's no one else there?'

'No one.'

'You said once you'd die for me.'

'I almost did.'

'I'm sorry.'

'I know. Me too. We'll ring you at eight in the morning, okay?'

'Okay. Goodnight.'

'Goodnight.'

They sit in a bright, clean restaurant and a smiling waitress comes and stands at their table.

'This young lady will have a burger and fries and a Sprite. And I'll have…could I just have a large salad?'

'My daddy is a vegetarian,' his daughter says.

'Is he, honey?'

'Yes. He was a vegetarian before I was born. Weren't you?'

He nods an embarrassed nod.

'This lady is busy, Lynn. She doesn't need my life story.'

'We saw a sea dragon last night on the beach and we put it back in the sea.'

'Well, ain't you the lucky girl. Been here all my life and I can't say I've seen one yet.'

'My daddy said I was lucky, too.'

'Your daddy's right.'

'And we saw a sand gull one day.'

'Wow. You're blessed!'

'Lynn,' he says, 'the lady is busy.'

'Are you busy?'

'Not so I can't hear about sea dragons and sand gulls,' she smiles a warm smile. 'But I'd better bring your Sprite or you're gonna run dry and then you won't be able to keep me entertained with your stories.'

The little girl giggles.

'And coffee for your dad?'

'Thank you.'

Later, they go to SafariLand but he finds he doesn't have the $25 they need to get in. The woman at the admission booth looks at the $19 he counts out and shrugs and listens to his explanation about having left his money in his other jeans.

'Sorry, honey. No mon, no fun.'

They walk slowly to the car.

'We'll come back another day.'

Across the hedges and fences they can see and hear the people on the water slides he promised he'd bring Lynn on. He knows she's upset but she doesn't cry.

When they get back to the apartment, they play chess in the afternoon heat and, as the sun begins to sink, they go down to the pool and his daughter takes her first, tentative strokes and he remembers the day she first walked.

Later still, they ramble to the edge of the woods and watch the fireflies do their flame dance and they catch one in a jar and bring it back to the apartment and when his daughter falls asleep he opens the jar and releases the fly into the darkness that's beginning to blow a storm.

They spend most of the following day at the pool. His daughter is frightened by the rolling breakers on the beach, by the pounding of the waves after the previous night's slow gale. Only in the early evening, when the sky is clear and the heat is clean and the sea has calmed, do they go walking on the beach.

Mostly, they have it to themselves. Five hundred yards ahead of them the surfers skim to a standstill and then turn and paddle out again, in search of a last few breaking waves, reminders of the previous night's turmoil.

He watches his daughter scrutinize the sea, nervous of whatever violence it still might hold. He inspects the pieces of flotsam and jetsam on the sand: a broken plastic fish box; three battered kerosene cans; a plank of yellow wood; dead fish, their mouths wide open in a series of silent cries, and what looks like a human heart.

For a moment, he cannot believe what he's seeing. His daughter has wandered ahead, dragging a piece of timber from the shallows; she is writing her name in the sand. A giant L and a tiny y and two ill-fitting 'n's.

Bending, he looks more closely and, yes, as far as he can tell, it is a human heart. He feels his own heart pound in his chest, its every throb a punch against his ribs. What to do: lift it and take it with him to the apartment? What then, call the police? Explain why he had moved it from its resting place?

'See my name?' his daughter calls.

'Yes, I see. That's very good.'

He walks to where she's standing, hoping that when he turns there will be no heart on the sand.

'Will I write your name?'

'Yes, do. Can you spell it?'

'Yep.'

She drags the piece of timber through the damp sand, slowly carving the two letters.

'And Mum's?'

'Yes.'

Again, she sets about the task, her tongue between her teeth, concentrating hard, working her way through the eight letters of her mother's name.

'Now,' she says, standing back.

'That's wonderful. You've done a great job.'

His daughter nods and hands him the piece of timber.

'Can we go back now? I'm hungry.'

'Of course.'

He steers her away from the waterline, away from the dark heart resting on the shore.

'Let's see if we can find a sand dollar on the way back.'

He sticks the piece of timber into the sand, well above the high watermark, an indicator for the morrow. For now, there is nothing he can do. He doesn't want to bring the heart to his daughter's attention, doesn't want to frighten her with this macabre gift from the sea.

That night he dreams the dream again. He sees himself, the second youngest man at the long table, hardly more than a boy. This is all he ever dreams. The reverie never takes him beyond this point and on to the other, darker days that followed. Instead, he sits with the others and someone begins to sing a soft song. He knows this bit of the dream has come from elsewhere, from another time and place, when they would sing together. It comes from one of the nights at a desert campfire or an evening in winter when they were crowded into one room in someone's house. But, in this dream, the singing happens at the long table. It starts at the other end, Andrew's voice running like a low, slow river beneath the conversation, gradually making its way into the ears of the listeners, stopping their speech until the song can run freely, without the word-rocks getting in its way, until each of them picks it up and feels the lightness of its beauty begin to lift them. Always the same dream and the same song that seems about to explode, to drive them from their seats and lead them smiling through the marshalled, silent streets outside. Forever, he sits waiting for someone else to rise; he waits to follow, he knows he will not lead. But the song never quite reaches that pinnacle. Instead, it fades away, the words becoming sparser, the silent gaps expanding to fill the moments between those words until, at last, there is only the silence, and the room is as it was that night, full of fear and indecision. And then he wakes, as he always does, his body a berg of perspiring skin, his hair dripping sweat into his open eyes.

Outside, he hears thunder rising and falling, catches the sheets of lighting through the window of his room and hears the wind begin to rise.

The following morning, he leaves his daughter with her new-found friend, Melissa, and Melissa's mother at the pool and jogs to the point where the timber marker still skewers the warm sand. His stomach is churning, bile rising in his throat. He tries to remember how far above the tidemark the heart was resting. He wishes it gone but he needs to be sure, needs to go back. If it is still there, he has no idea what he'll do. Chances are the tide or a scavenging gull will have lifted it, yet it doesn't matter if the heart is there or gone. What matters is the fact that it was there.

The sea is calm, the tide retreating steadily. And, indeed, the heart has disappeared. He walks fifty yards in each direction, scanning the sand and the shallows but no sign of it remains. The surge of the sea or some wandering foragers have done their work and there is no longer what Ken might call a situation requiring resolution.

Standing in the shallows, Al vomits, the clear water diluting the green liquid, sucking it out into the deeper waves and the open ocean beyond.

That afternoon they drive to SafariLand. To his relief, the woman at the box office is not the woman who turned them away. Inside, the park is virtually empty. He counts five people on the paths between the rides.

'Right,' he says. 'Where would you like to start – water slide, roundabout, bumper cars, dinosaur, elephant swing?'

'Can we do them all?'

'We can do them all. We have all afternoon. Twice if you like.'

She laughs.

'Really?'

'Really.'

'Mum would love this, wouldn't she?'

'She would.'

'Can we come here some time with her?'

'Let's hope we can.'

And now he sits in his car. It is late in the afternoon and the last of the autumn light is being tightly wrung from the heavens, dribbling down onto the flaky, rusted stubble of a long, wide field. He watches an old crow flail jadedly across the dull September sky, in search of its rookery, and he thinks of his daughter running carelessly along the sprawling summer paths of the amusement park, her sun-bleached hair flying like a thousand short kite strings in the brightness.

And he remembers the shadow of a gull on the warm summer sand.

And the sacred hearts of those he loved and lost.

Say to Your Brother

The strange thing was, the night before my brother came to take me to the opera house, I had a dream about him. In the dream, I was looking through the rain-drenched windscreen of his car and he was sitting in the driver's seat with the barrel of a gun in his mouth and I knew he was going to kill himself; that it wasn't an idle threat. And that was the totality of the dream. Nothing else happened in it. I stood in the pouring rain in the car park of an industrial estate, outside a wholesale framing office, and he sat in his car, the pistol in his hand, the barrel in his mouth, each of us waiting for him to pull the trigger, this sheet of glass and rain between us and, in the dream, the perspective kept changing. Some of the time I could see what was happening from my point of view and some of the time from his.

He insisted on driving me out to the opera house. I could have taken a train or a taxi but he wouldn't hear of it. He was adamant about picking me up at the apartment and taking me out there.

He didn't talk a lot on the journey and whenever I turned to speak to him, I could see the perspiration glinting on his forehead.

'You all right?'

'I'm okay.'

'Want me to drive?'

'No, I'm fine. Tell me again, what are you going out here for?'

'I need to look at some scenery they have in their store. We may be able to borrow it for our own play.'

'Right.'

'But it may be too big, too awkward. I'm just checking.'

'In which case?'

'In which case it's back to a black box.'

'Not for the first time,' he said, laughing, and I noticed a dribble of saliva like dark lava on his chin. He wiped it away roughly with the palm of his hand and dropped back into silence, his hands gripping hard on the wheel.

'You mind if I turn the radio on?'

'Something easy,' he said quietly.

'I can leave it off.'

'No, it's fine. Just something easy though – nothing raucous.'

'I doubt your car radio can receive raucous,' I said.

Easing through the stations, I came on one that played light classical.

'That'll do,' my brother said. 'That's good.'

Someone was singing the Bailero.

'Sublime,' he said, very softly.

'And obscure.'

'Only to you, brother.'

'Meaning?'

'*Pastré, lou prat fai flour, li cal*
Gorda toun troupel!
Dio lou bailero lero, lero, lero, bailero, lo!
L'erb es pu fin' ol prat d'oici.
Shepherd, the meadow is in bloom,

89

Come over here to sing the Bailero.

The grass is greener on this side.'

I wasn't sure whether he had simply misunderstood my question or chosen to misunderstand it.

'Simple,' I said.

'But beautiful for that.'

'True.'

We drove on, out along the coast road. Someone, in a fit of madness or brilliance, had decided to build the opera house twelve miles outside the city, on a cliff overlooking the ocean. Getting there was a pleasure in itself, the sun sharpening and filing the blue of the water away to our left, its glint razoring the mid-morning.

'Beautiful,' my brother said, glancing out the car window. 'Do you miss it?'

I shook my head. 'Not in the slightest. I was never very comfortable with it, anyway. If I never saw it again, it wouldn't worry me.'

'But it is beautiful.'

'Not necessarily beautiful when you're on it. It can turn. I never trusted it. Even when it was calm, it had a way of turning. "Never trust the smile of the sea," Peter used to say.'

'Like life.'

'Who are you telling?'

'Do you miss him?' my brother asks.

'Can't say I do. Sometimes wonder where he got to and what happened to him – you know that kind of thing – but only occasionally. It all seems like another life, another world. Times are better now; life is better here.'

We slid back into our individual silences.

After a while, I took a sheet of paper from my shirt pocket and checked, for the twentieth time, the measurements of our available theatre space. To have an actual set that wasn't simply an array of crates or pallets or chipboard boxes would be an achievement in itself. Not that a set guarantees an audience but it does at least allow the audience something to look at and, given the kinds of obscure and difficult plays we were producing then, that would come as some relief to our few paying customers.

'You enjoy this design stuff?'

'I do.'

'That's good.'

The sea faded as we wound inland for a couple of miles, its colours and textures lightening and running in the harsh sunlight, becoming a sheet of faded blotting paper. The radio was playing something fast.

'What's that?' I asked.

'Ignorance,' my brother sighed. 'Chopin. Minute Waltz. But it's not.'

'Not what?'

'A minute,' he laughed. 'Just in case you're timing it.'

'Right.'

'You don't like it.'

'No.'

'Taste. Or the absence thereof.'

He was smiling but his smile faded as another gob of dark saliva trickled down his chin. He wiped it away; I pretended not to notice.

And then we rounded a sharp bend and the opera house materialized, a glisten of refraction and reflection on a broad headland, and beyond and through it the full expanse of the ocean.

'That's what you get for twenty-eight million,' I said.

'Worth every penny.'

'Only if their set fits our stage.'

'You, brother, are a true philistine,' he said, bringing the car to a halt overlooking the sea.

'You want to come in, have a coffee or something?'

'No, I'm fine here. I'll wait for you.'
'Shouldn't be too long. It fits or it doesn't.'
'Take your time.'

Inside, the foyer of the opera house was a dizzy dance of light and colour, pulling the cobalt of the sea through the glass walls, its light spilling across the steel-grey tiles. I thought of our own dark, damp-smelling, cramped little theatre and I missed it.

'May I help you?' the receptionist asked.
'I have an appointment with your designer.'
'Technical, lighting, wardrobe, creative or print?'
'I'm here about a set.'
She nodded disinterestedly and picked up a phone.
'Name?'
'John. From the Pearl.'
'The Pearl?'
'Theatre.'
Another casual nod.
'Martin. A gentleman from the Pearl Theatre. Yes, I understand.' She put down the phone. 'He's on his way. If you'd like to take a seat.'
'Thank you.'
'My pleasure.'
I doubted it.

The set was too big and anyway, once I saw it, I realised it was all wrong for our dark little spot, and I was almost relieved.

'Sorry about that,' Martin shrugged. 'If there are any bits and pieces I can help you with, just let me know. Mountains of stuff here that'll never be used again.'
'Thanks.'
'These kinds of sets don't transfer easily. They're built for here. Scale. Gaudiness. Bloody weight. But who am I telling?

You already know all that. Sometimes I look at the waste in here and it makes me want to puke.'

I thought of my brother outside in his car, the trickles and dribbles of blood in his spit, and I thanked Martin and turned to leave.

'You fancy a cappuccino or something?'

'There's someone waiting for me outside.'

'Bring them in!'

'Thanks but he'll want to get going. And, listen, thanks for showing me the stuff. I really appreciate it.'

'Anytime. You guys are doing good work.'

Back outside, the late morning heat was rising. My brother's car appeared to be empty. I scanned the car park and the steps of the opera house but there was no sign of him. I imagined he'd wandered down to sit in the shade of the trees near the cliff. I doubted he'd gone too far.

I came out onto the path that led to a seating area overlooking the ocean. I expected to find him there, relaxing in the shade of the recently planted trees that had been bought in fully grown, but there was no sign of him. There really wasn't anywhere else for him to go.

I climbed back up to the car park, thinking he might have returned or left a note on the windscreen. Only when I reached the car, and glanced inside, did I see him curled in the foetal position on the back seat. His skin was the bark of silver beech, and, despite the iron heat of the day, he was shivering.

Pulling open the front door, I knelt on the driver's seat and leaned over him.

'You okay?'

He shook his head.

'I'll drive you to the hospital,' I said quickly.

Again, he shook his head.

'Ambulance,' he whispered hoarsely.

I found my mobile and dialled.

While we waited, he remained lying on the back seat, curled like an animal dying in pain. His fingers were locked gears about his knees, blue bones tearing his ashen skin, his face an olive shade of white, his hair and shirt sweat-soaked.

'Why did you insist on driving me out here?'

'Thought I'd be okay.'

A car drew up and someone got out and went inside the opera house.

'Time is short,' my brother said.

'How short?'

'Very.'

He paused, searching for words and breath. I thought a small smile crossed his mouth but I might have been mistaken. Perhaps it was the light or my anxiety.

'It was good,' he said at last.

'Yes?'

'To be with you.'

I nodded.

'The ambulance will be here soon. I'll come with you.'

'You drive my car.'

'I can come back for it later.'

'No. I'm going to be sick in that ambulance. Don't want you seeing that; don't want you there for that. Just follow in the car. Please.'

'Okay,' I said. 'Can I get you some water? Anything?'

He shook his head. The ambulance siren wept somewhere along the coast road. I knew my brother needed it to be here but I didn't want it to arrive.

'We should have gone home,' he said quietly. 'We should have gone back to where we belong. Both of us.'

I drove behind the ambulance, cranking through the gears, trying to make out the form of the paramedic, wanting to know if she was sitting by my brother's side or standing over him, holding his hand or administering oxygen, but I couldn't see anything through the small, opaque windows. Nothing beyond the bolted doors with their urgent lettering.

For a while, the sea was an occasional glimmer on my right, an irritation in the corner of my field of vision. Then we turned to face into the sun, and the shadow of the ambulance acted as a shield, its silhouette falling onto the dusty windscreen.

'Yea, though I walk through the valley of the shadow of death, I will fear no evil,' I said out loud and, as I spoke, the ambulance swung left and the sun was in my face again, my eyes tightening in its glare, wishing the precious miles away.

And then we were on the outskirts of the city, weaving through the light traffic, switching lanes, and I was tailgating the ambulance through red lights, cursing those who cursed me, trying to ignore the blinking fuel warning light, making bets with some God – if the petrol doesn't run out before we reach the hospital, he'll be all right. And I thought I heard whatever God it was sniggering quietly, and I knew I was a fool.

My brother's room in the hospital was a cool, safe, shaded place. It took some time before they let me see him. He had, as he'd predicted, been sick in the ambulance and then, again, in the hospital room but by the time the door was opened to me, the nurses had done their job and the place smelled only of cleanliness.

'He's good,' a young nurse said. 'A bit woozy but he's good. Resting.'

She smiled a professional smile, nodding to my brother and then to me, her bottom lip protruding slightly to cradle the upper one, but her eyes were alive with humanity and I hoped that was something we both could trust.

'There's a call button just there,' she told me. 'Don't hesitate to use it. I'll be back soon.'

'Thank you.'

The door swung gently behind her.

'So here we are,' my brother said quietly. 'In one piece. How was the car?'

'Good. Fine. Low on petrol but it got me here.'

'I'll let you give it the next fill.'

'You're not getting away with that one,' I laughed. 'You can fill it when you get out.'

He smiled a knowing smile and I felt foolish at my pretence.

'The car is yours,' he said. 'If you don't want to keep it, you can sell it.'

'I'll be really glad to have it. Thanks.'

'I hated that fucking ambulance. I'm always sick in ambulances.'

'You've been in one before?'

'Today was my…' He counted slowly on his fingers, remembering. 'Sixth trip. And sick on every one.'

'You never told me.'

A wry smile, a twist of the mouth, a shrug.

'You're comfortable?'

'Yes.'

I sat in the armchair by his bed. He closed his eyes and his breathing became quieter, rested and restful; the easy rhythm made me happy for him. Seeing his washed-out features, it was hard to believe that two hours before he'd been driving me along the coast, ill but functioning.

'You're still there?' he asked. His eyes remained closed.

'Yes. Not going anywhere.'

'Good.'

He looked about him, taking a few seconds to focus, his eyes slowly searching the room.

'All these people,' he said quietly.

'What people?'

'In a shadow ring around me. The living and the dead.'

'There's just you and me here, brother. Just us.'

'Really?'

'Yes.'

His brow furrowed and he closed his eyes again and, when he spoke, his voice leaked out in a whisper.

'My bags are packed. I'm ready for the journey.'

'Are you?'

There was no reply. The corner of his mouth had sagged into a broken arc.

'We'll monitor the situation,' the nurse said. 'Hard to tell at this stage.'

'But it's not looking good?'

'No, it's not looking good.'

'I can stay?'

'Of course. We're going to do tests. You might like to get some air, have something to eat. Come back in thirty minutes. We'll be done by then.'

ii

There's a pencil of light from the gap where the hospital door is slightly ajar, just enough for me to write these lines for you, my brother. You're sleeping, your lungs are opened and closed and opened and closed by machinery. The shadow of my hand is falling across this page – just as the shadow of something darker, something a lot less certain, is falling over your damaged body.

I want to comfort you; I want to be the reassuring one, as you so often have been to me. I want to come out from the shadow of the older brother and take charge of this situation. I want to tell you everything will be all right but I know it won't. And if you could talk, you'd tell me that, too. You're the one who'd know exactly what's happening and why.

You were the one who always found a way round things but you'd be the first to tell me there's no way round this.

In your car, on the drive from the opera house to the hospital, I heard Elton John singing from the radio in the warm summer air, telling the story of Daniel.

Dearest brother, only brother, I love you. I love you for all the days we shared and all the times we were apart. Your kindness was a soft voice down the telephone line, telling me things would work out fine, that there was no point in worrying. I wish I could say the same for you and know there was some truth in it. Instead, the night draws on and the moon retreats a degree or two and we share this room, as we once shared a room at home – you talking in one bed, me laughing in the other.

Now we're both silent but for the drive and draw of the machine pumping air into your wounded lungs and the soft sound of my pen crossing the pages of what's left of our life together.

I close my eyes and hear the echo of your words and the memory of my laughter and Elton John's song coming in on the late-night radio, its notes drifting across the empty car park, its tenderness hanging in the slow summer night.

iii

I'm driving down the warm summer roads, heading for the coast.

You're a week dead, brother, and I'm driving your car. I sit back in your seat and let the sun pour over me. The hot air is blowing through the open windows. You'd laugh if you could see me. You'd tell me there's not much point in having air-conditioning if I'm going to drive with the windows open. You'd tell me I'm a loola.

I know all that. I look in the rear view mirror and I see your eyes looking back at me and I wink and, immediately, you know there's no point in lecturing me about air-conditioning. I'll do what I'm doing and there's nothing you can say that'll stop me. To be brutally honest with you, I'm hoping the summer wind will blow some of the chill out of my body and out of whatever it is that I think of as my soul. I'm hoping it'll put some warmth back in my heart. Seven days of waiting for the mist to lift, seven days of waking up to the fact that you're dead, seven days of freezing in the hundred degree heat.

I think I'm turning on the car radio but it's set to CD and I find myself listening to the last music you listened to, as you drove back up this coast road a few weeks ago. This is the music you chose to hear, even though you knew you were dying. These are the songs that brought you home from that weekend at the beach. And here they are playing, again, playing for me as I retrace the miles you drove.

I listen to all those hits from the sixties. A time when you were young and I was younger and we both had so much to live for. Some of the songs I remember from the 45s that appeared at Christmas and summer, in the weeks when you were home. I'd sit on the couch and listen to them and, when you weren't there, I'd play them again and turn them over and listen to the B-sides, learn the words so that I'd have them to sing when you'd gone back to college. They were yours and that meant something to me.

Some I barely remember and some I can hear you singing and I turn up the volume and I drive that bit faster and the warm wind is blowing everything away except the sound of the songs and the sound of your voice and those eyes that keep catching mine in the mirror above me.

iv

The last time I walked along this beach, you were walking with me. It was late in the evening and the sun was settling into the sea beyond the Point. We were talking about the past. We were laughing. And then the conversation grew more serious. It turned to talk of childhood and how our memories differed. I was telling you how important it was to me to have an older brother, how I always felt safe when you were around, how I missed you when you went back to school, when you went away to college, when you left to live abroad.

But there were things I didn't tell you that evening. I didn't tell you that I felt I was always five steps behind you. I didn't tell you how wonderful it was for me that the last five years had drawn us closer together than we'd ever been before, brought us eventually to the same city. I didn't tell you how I looked forward to those weekly phone calls, those daily emails, the meals together, your healthy cynicism, the closeness that overcame everything. I didn't tell you how much I loved you.

I wish now that I had said all that. I wish I'd opened my heart more to you, but that's not the way I am, that's not my style, as you well knew.

So here I am, walking the beach again, alone this time. The evening sand is still hot under my feet, the small waves that break around my ankles are warm. This is summer, this is America, this is your beach and up there is the place that was home to you between May and September.

I reach the Point, that spot at the end of the island where there is only sea. Daylight is being sucked down into the waves, fading quickly, as it always does out here. A full moon is rising through the haze that hangs above the ocean.

Turning, I see that the beach is empty and I retrace my steps, as we did that evening two years ago. The buoys keep calling your name through the summer night, tolling its two syllables, out there in the misted light of the moon. Just beyond the place where my eyes can be sure of what I see.

Listen! There they are again. And again. And again. Across the water and eastward to home.

v

The cabin lights have dimmed. Around me, I watch heads nodding and lolling in uneasy sleep. The sound of the aircraft engines is a constant lullaby. Someone passes, in search of a cup of coffee, and smiles.

I picture you, my brother, on a flight like this, cruising through the night on your way back home to bury our father. That was six years ago. I know he would gladly have given a decade of his life to have you live another healthy year.

We walked together, the three of us, you, our sister and myself, behind his coffin, stopping at the gate of the house where we grew up. Smiling at the separate and mutual memories of that place and those days. We were together, sharing the end of a life but we were together, too, in facing what we believed was the future. We were family.

Back then, you guessed nothing of your silent sickness. Or, if you had your suspicions, you said nothing.

And now, with Europe dawning through the aircraft window, I can't even begin to imagine what you thought and how you felt when they told you. Not that you needed telling; this was your job. You, who had spent your days bringing life into the world, knew exactly what to expect from the leaving of it. Physician, heal thyself!

With the black Atlantic 37,000 feet below us, I imagine you somewhere down there, the true believer, in the coracle of your soul.

You're the two weeks that have passed since you died ahead of me, making steady progress through the waves, towards the shores of Ireland. You stop when you make land on Inis Mór, resting up a day or two and then you're off again, on the last push for home.

You travel faster now, between the stone walls of Connaught. The sea is only a memory. The sea is almost forgotten and, as you cross through midland fields, the landscape becomes, suddenly, familiar. Each gateway, every twist and tree summons a memory from this other life, the one where I am still flying in this aeroplane, seven miles above the earth. And I know exactly where you are: you're waiting in the shelter of the porch at the back of the church in our village. The soil there remembers you and keeps a place for you, our earth, your earth, your home.

vi

It's a month since your death, brother, and I hear your name on the obits of the local radio station, reminding me, as if I need reminding, that it's two days to your burial. The countryside is golden brown, like the song. The crops are poised for harvesting. The field beyond this ditch is already stubbled, waiting for the torch to flame from headland to headland. Ashes to ashes, dust to swirling dust. Your ashes melting back into the clay of home.

I look at the photograph on the wall. It's six years, to the day, since it was taken. There you are, laughing in the face of everything. You have your jacket hooked across your shoulder. Your sunglasses reflect the light of the burning day and the clear blue sky. Our shirts are the white of lilies. You and me, best man and groom, brother and brother, happy together. Six years ago to the day.

And here on my desk, book-marking someone's poems, is a postcard you sent me from Savannah. It's like a dream among all the other dreams.

'We can hit Savannah some weekend and Charleston. Think you would enjoy.'

All the plans you'd made for that trip. You were going to show me the places that were important to you. You were going to play 'Moon River' in the car. You were telling me I had to read *Midnight in the Garden of Good and Evil* before I came over. You were emailing me maps and itineraries. You were saying, 'Come on, don't wait, come this spring.' But I didn't – I put it off for six months, a year and, by then, it was too late.

The Angel Said

I sit at the small table and eat my breakfast, wondering, as I wonder every morning, where my brother is. I ask myself the questions I ask first thing each morning and last thing each night. Is Peter alive? Will we ever find each other again? Does he wish to meet or has too much icy water flowed under the bridges of experience? Then I wonder if he's well and if he's enjoying his life greatly or to some extent or at all. And then I stop this gradation of life, this slotting of emotions into pockets.

I wish him only happiness.

I don't wonder if he thinks of me.

And then I finish my breakfast and watch the passing shapes of the figures in the street – quavers and semi-quavers with crochets in tow; figures of darkness and, occasionally, figures blessed by the light of the falling snow.

Once my morning meal is over, I go and wash in the small bathroom that is never bright and never warm. Snow piles halfway up the thick little windowpane in winter and pigeons squat there, blocking and unblocking the light with their comings and goings all year round. In winter I stop shaving; it's easier that way. My beard sprouts in all directions and for those few months I can imagine that I might have been born here, might be one of these people and not an interloper from somewhere beyond the Black Sea.

In the small room that houses my bed and my instruments and music, I perform my little ritual of tidying, as I do every morning, carefully straightening the sheets, punching my pillows into shape. I take my violin from its case, randomly choose a piece of sheet music – probably the only random thing I will do in any day – and place it on the music stand. I pause and then play the chosen piece through twice, before carefully replacing my violin in its case and putting the sheet music back in its ordered spot.

Beyond the window, in the cemetery, young boys are throwing snowballs, dodging behind the headstones, squatting in the shelter of small crosses before launching their next attack on each other. Their voices come faintly across the ledgered lines of memorials, some as dour as those they commemorate; some sporting bowed ribbons for the season of the living; a few splashed with the petals of winter flowers. Two young girls in short skirts and skimpy tops stand at the gate of the cemetery watching until the boys, in a show of bluster drive them, laughing, back onto the living street.

I leave the room, closing the door behind me, and complete the other odds and ends that need doing – making sandwiches, washing my cup and plate before putting on a coat, scarf and hat and leaving my apartment for the short walk to the church where I work as choirmaster.

I am a creature of habit. Perhaps I was always so, though I like to think there were weeks and even months when I was otherwise, the weeks and months when Peter was about.

There is a young boy sitting on the narrow stairs of his parents' house. It is late in the night; more than late, it is the early hours of the morning. The boy sits in the most uncomfortable position possible, his back arched and aching, his hands clasped tightly about his knees, his fingers welded painfully together. He does not move. His pyjamas are thin and the night is cold, but he wants to suffer. He hopes that he can barter with God, swap his discomfort for his parents' happiness. If he sits here for another sixteen minutes and forty seconds, if he counts to a thousand – slowly – then the arguing will end, peace will flutter through the winter window like the angel of the Lord and happiness will, at last, be tangible. Despite his youth, he understands the meaning of the word tangible.

What he doesn't understand, though he has an intimation of it, is why he is being used as a shield in a marriage that seems incapable of generating anything but anger and discontent. Even he, a boy of ten, can see how much better life would be for everyone if the voices from the kitchen were to move elsewhere, one to one end of the village, one to the other. But, instead, the war goes on, and his welfare is invoked as a justification by both parents.

If it wasn't for....

Well I'm not going to walk out and leave....

An intermediary without power, the phrase pops like an organ stop as I'm locking the door at the foot of the stairs.

That is what I was. An ineffective go-between, my role defined by those who needed to justify themselves.

'Without power or respect,' I add out loud.

A passing figure looks up, frowns an even deeper frown and then returns his eyes to the frozen snow that pleats the footpath. I turn my key a third time and the lock creaks into place. I try the door: locked, tight.

I look up, as I do every morning at the massive edifice that is my workplace. It sits like a great bird, its profile moving slowly across the summer days, its darkness a permanence on the winter skyline. Nothing in this part of the city can exist without this reference pile impinging on its being. No one who lives in this quarter can get into or out of bed without its real or imagined shadow gouging a deep, slow path across their dreams and imaginings.

The young boy, who sat on the winter stairs, stands at the edge of the sea. The late summer sun is bending and creasing the horizon in shades of red and orange and ochre and he knows that it will hardly be gone from one sky before it pushes into the other sky, sidling above the morning mountains.

As yet, the rising dread as his brother's departure approaches has not become the uppermost thought in the young boy's head. He is happy in the knowledge that the dark shape in the crimson water is his brother's punt, moving between the lobster pots, and that before the sun has gone down Peter will be stepping from that small boat into the water and he will rush to help. They will paddle through the shallows, each with a hand on the light gunwale, lifting the boat clear of the sea, leaving a track on the pale sand as they drag it above the tidemark.

'Good man,' his brother will say. 'Only for you.'

'You'd have got it clear on your own.'

'But together we're better.'

The phrase will stick in his mind. The phrase will become his mantra and will keep him afloat in the days after Peter has gone back to his naval training.

'I like when you're here,' the young boy says, uncertainly.

His brother turns the punt over and it lies like a turtle on the sand.

'I know. It's tough for you. Being here with them when they're like this. But it probably seems a lot worse for you. I don't think they even notice that they're arguing. It's a way of life for them. They'd miss it if they couldn't bicker.'

His brother smiles but the young boy feels a frozen rock lodged in his stomach.

'Hey, I'm not gone yet,' Peter laughs. 'Let's do something tomorrow. Let's take the sailboat out and have a picnic and when we get back we'll go to the cinema. A day away, just the two of us, all day. We'll get up early, be gone before they're even awake. Okay?'

The young boy smiles a big smile and his brother puts his arm around him and they do the elephant walk all the way up the beach.

I make my way, as I do each morning, through the cemetery, wandering between the stones, walking every path. I have my own reason for taking this circuitous route. It's not to familiarise myself with the faces and names and dates on the monuments; nor is it the strange attraction of the military section of the burial ground – though I always stop there and consider the remarkable cholera of loss with which the twentieth century infected this country: the Great War; the Revolution; the Second World War, an infection that recurred with devastating consequences.

But it's not this remembered wretchedness that is the object of my morning walk. My stopping is simply a way to justify the other daily stop I make, putting it in the safe keeping of the routine. If I linger among the war dead, then why should I not stop, too, at the grave of Nikolai Kalinnikov? If one is habit, why should the other not be just the same?

Sometimes my caution angers me. Why should a choirmaster not stop to remember his choirboy? Why should one human being require an excuse to linger at the grave of another? What is it that I fear?

Nikolai Kalinnikov will have been resting here for two years in one month's time. His anniversary is bearing down upon us and we will remember him in word and music when the day comes round and I, perhaps, will remember him more than most. His burning eyes and sweet laughter, his constant energy and sense of fun, that occasional and guarded smile that was the antithesis of laughter. A smile that was as infrequent as it was promising.

Other than in the course of my duties, I doubt I spoke personally to Nikolai more than a dozen times in the almost three years we spent together as teacher and pupil. But when I did, I saw a different person, not the wild young thing who was always rushing; not the urchin who laughed at every joke; not the boy who was forever involved in pranks, and not the chorister whose voice was deeply beautiful. I saw a child becoming a young man; eyes that were intense and a smile that asked and promised everything.

I loved Nikolai Kalinnikov. Not with some seedy, leering intent. Not with thoughts of touching or being touched by him. Not with the intention of his sleeping in my bed, but with a love that made me happy and sought only for his happiness. I never laid a finger on his skin, never kissed his face, never considered such possibilities and yet something in that enigmatic smile made me believe that he might some day kiss my mouth, touch my skin, that he might suggest we lie together in a distant future – not here but, perhaps, on the warmer shores of my own country.

And then, one bitter morning two winters ago, he leapt, as he always did, from the open door of the city tram as it slowed on the corner beside the church. Not for Nikolai the one-minute walk from the next stop.

So he leapt, as he always leapt, running to keep pace with the tram before making the safety of the footpath. I had seen him do it many times but I wasn't there that morning to watch his legs go from under him and his knees buckle as the tram unexpectedly picked up speed. He slipped – not for the first time – and skidded on the packed ice beside the tram tracks, but on this occasion, rather than tumbling harmlessly, he slid across the ice, body spinning until the force of his skull against the pavement kerb brought his fall and his life to an end.

I saw his body that afternoon. Two of us teachers were dispatched to formally identify his remains, to spare his parents the trauma. Ironically, we travelled on the very tram from which he had slipped. Someone had placed a small bouquet of winter evergreens on the rear platform.

In the hospital we were led to the dismal morgue where Nikolai lay beneath an icy sheet. His handsome young face had barely been scratched by the packed ice, but it had been grazed by death, and I wondered whether that kind of death is any less demeaning than if his features had been burned by the sharpness of the ice. His vigorous body looked out of place in that charnel house and I thought of another emaciated body, that of a young man who had survived at another time and in a different place, and I was perplexed.

Often on summer evenings, when the young boy's older brother was away fishing on one or other of the half-dozen trawlers based in the small harbour close to their home, he would walk down to the dock wall and stare at the distant horizon, willing the trawler bow to slice through the evening mist. And sometimes a trawler would appear and the young boy would patrol the low wall, wishing the hull to be red or blue or yellow, depending on which boat his brother had shipped on.

And once, once only, when the boy was at the harbour, the hull was red, as he had hoped, and his brother brought him on board and allowed him to assist with the unloading.

'You have a good helper there, Peter,' one of the trawler men had said.

'None better,' his brother had replied, tousling his hair and smiling at him, and the young boy had felt a pedestal rise beneath his feet and wished he could travel for ever in the light of his brother's shadow.

But more often the young boy is sitting at the kitchen table in the silence. From outside come the sounds of summer children at play and then the silence is broken by his father's booming rant about something or other that is of no importance, and the young boy sits and listens but he does not hear. He is watching the notes that climb slowly and slide quietly, up and down the stairway of the treble clef. And as his father's voice becomes intolerably loud, the young boy recites the words that cast a spell, silencing his father's spitting tongue – tonic solfa; stave; staff; ledger; space; brace; rest; interval; quaver; semiquaver; demisemiquaver; hemidemisemiquaver.

And he hears his mother say: 'I'm not sitting here if you two can't be civil to each other' and he's tempted to smile because he hasn't spoken a word but he doesn't smile because that would bring his father's palm crashing against the side of his face and leave his eardrum ringing. Instead, he satisfies himself with the knowledge that there is no one who can disturb the words inside his head because no one can hear their soft hum and their sharp jingle or see the way they wind about each other, one touching the next and that, in turn, caressing the next. Tonic solfa – he loves the warm encouragement of the word tonic, the way it says wellness. It touches him like his mother's hand touches his forehead when he has a winter fever, with sureness and compassion, telling him everything will be all right. The word is there for him, as she would be. Then there's the sharper sound of the word solfa. When he sees the word, he sees an axe head and then a very short handle and the axe head is of a gleaming, steely silver. It rests in the comfortable arc of his father's skull. Around the silver head there's a pool of quiet blood, fresh but not flowing. His father is sitting calmly in an armchair, the axe lodged in his cranium. He is watching television and the young boy knows his father will never shout again, never raise his hand in anger. The axe has dulled his viciousness and made him content to sit and watch whatever tripe the set beams at him. And everything is peaceful in the house. Tonic solfa, he thinks but he doesn't forget himself; he doesn't smile or invite the violence of the real world into the serenity of his imagination.

But sometimes he sits on the cold stairway, wishing his father would strike him, wishing his scalded skin, his shaken jawbone, the burning in his ear, the pain in his head could replace the words and tears pouring up through the dark floor of the sad, brutal world. Believing that one act of acceptance on his part, one rain of blows might wash away the stale stink of anger and frustration that hangs about the house like the smell of rotting fish. He would willingly sacrifice his eardrum or his jawbone or the straightness of his nose or the sight in his eye for an end to this cacophony. And, in the dark of night, the magic words become nothing more than a collection of letters, ineffective and useless. Space; brace; rest; interval; quaver. Mere words.

There is a photograph of Nikolai Kalinnikov in the corridor behind the church altar. It hangs in a space shaded by two pillars, so that his beautiful, smiling face peers from the shadows and seems just beyond reach.

One afternoon, some jostling boys dislodged it from its hook and shattered the glass in the plain timber frame. I volunteered to have the glass repaired and, at the same time, had the photograph copied. I put the copy carefully in the sheet music of Tchaikovsky's 'Happy is the Man' in my bedroom.

Occasionally, when by chance I pull that piece of music from the shelf and play it through, I spend a moment or two looking closely at the face of the boy I loved. Love.

Otherwise, I try not to catch his eye in the gloomy church corridor. I prefer to imagine his voice among the voices of the young men hurrying to choir practice. And, as they crowd into the rehearsal room, I keep my eyes firmly on my roll-book.

'Gentlemen,' I say quietly and they fall silent and some of them smile and some are clearly concentrating and some simply wait in that great silence that precedes the music we shall sing together.

Once, when the young boy was a young man and was travelling in his brother's company, and in the company of other young men, they were crossing a choppy sea in a small sailboat and the waves were high and the night was dark and no one seemed sure if the boat would float or sink. Peter came and sat by him and put his arm around him and whispered: 'Do you remember the night we went out in the punt to check the lines and we pretended there was a storm and we rocked the life out of the old flat-bottom?'

'Yes,' the young man says.

'Well tonight is just like that. All these other guys are terrified. You and me are the only ones who know it's all a joke. We know we're not going to sink, but let's not tell them,' and then Peter delivered a conspiratorial pat to encourage him to mask his terror.

'What's going on?' John, one of the other young men, asks. Even in the darkness his face is a moon of fear.

'Nothing going on, just talking,' the young man says.

'Are we sinking? Is this thing in trouble?'

'No trouble. Peter has it all under control.'

'You're not just saying that.'

'We've been out in worse, him and me, and survived. We'll be all right.'

'I don't understand you sea-people,' John says, his voice a little calmer. 'I'll bet you can't even swim. I've heard that about sea-people – they don't learn to swim; it only prolongs the agony of drowning.'

'I can swim,' the young man says. 'I think I swam before I walked. Stop worrying. Peter will get us safely across.'

'I hope you're right.'

And the young man smiles in the darkness because he has been infected with his brother's optimism and belief; they have shared something private and personal. Even in the midst of all these other people, the threshing of the waves and the slap and scream of the straining boat-timbers no longer frighten him and he turns his face into the rain and laughs quietly.

Occasionally, when I'm relaxing after choir practice, sitting over a steaming mug of tea, and I hear one of the choir-boys in the corridor singing a pop song he has heard on the radio, I think of the Captain and his love of music.

I was the first one in our town to fall under his spell but it wasn't his music that cast it, though it was his singing that first caught my attention. I heard him perform at a reading in the back room of a coffee shop. His singing was harmless, in tune but lacking any power or subtlety – bland is the word that best describes it. At the time, he'd sing only his own songs and they, too, were bland, without identifiable tunes and lyrically nothing better than rhyming propaganda. But when he spoke, between the songs, and when he told stories, it was an entirely different experience. The words and images drew you in, taking you to the place about which he spoke. For me, it was like being back at the silent table in my boyhood kitchen. The words he used echoed the words and images I had used to keep my father's anger at bay. They were different but their effect was the same. They had the power to render the present obsolete and make what he was saying the only reality that mattered.

It was the stories and the characters that peopled them that made his words electric. When he talked of someone he had met in a village square and what that person had said or done, I was there. The sun was toasting my back and the hot sand was caught between my sandalled toes. I was sitting on the low wall of a well. The cup he handed me was filled with clear, cold water and, as I drank from it, I felt a freshness and a cleanliness that made it different from the bottled water of the city bars and cafés.

And it had to do with more than taste or smell. It was filled with the possibilities that suddenly fell into my lap, the thought that everything need not always be the same; the notion that the generals, whose nailed boots dug into our shoulders, would not always be in charge; the belief that freedom was not a delusion. Belief was the key – I had believed in Peter when I was a boy, known that his presence would protect me from violence, silence and noise. And now there was someone else in whom I could believe, a man who was telling me that things could change and would change. His faith was infectious, his words beyond denial.

On Friday nights, after the folk club had closed, we'd go back, ten or fifteen of us, to the Captain's house and play music and swap songs. And sometimes, when the Captain sang, I'd strum his guitar and play the harmonica. Once or twice I put tunes to his words and we'd struggle over the compromises of song-writing until the sun came up, reminding us that we had work to do.

I was a music student then and the Captain was not yet the man he would soon become. The charisma was there and the stories were there but he hadn't quite found his direction.

Peter was living in a village just over an hour from the city. He had married and had children, built a boat shed, got into building and repairing boats. He still fished but only to feed his family and to supplement his income from the boat-building. I took him to see and hear the Captain a couple of times and I knew, very quickly, that he was as impressed as I was – more so, even.

After a couple of months, I began to recognise that the Captain's forte was as an entertainer and the nature of the music he enjoyed was different from the music I love. Music was a means for the Captain; it is an end for me.

I was still intrigued by his stories but I could see an emerging pattern. The characters became less important, the message more so. The group of friends who had gathered around him began to solidify, Peter at the helm. I stayed within the group, more out of habit than out of the commitment that Peter and Jude and some of the others possessed. Perhaps I stayed because Peter was such an integral part of the whole thing and leaving would have seemed, to me at least, like a betrayal.

Mostly, now, when I think of those days, it is as an adjunct to memories of my brother and to the recurring question of whether or not I will ever see him again. He had been my saviour and, as I grew up and moved out of the fear of my father's pathetic need for control, as I began my musical studies, in the holidays when I went to stay with Peter and his wife and their children and watched him at work in his boat shed, I recognised how much I owed him. And the only thing I could do to repay him was to sit on the porch of his house and play the sad songs he loved on the harmonica.

Now, all these years later, I regularly wake sweating, the source of my certainty gone. I get out of my bed, strip it of its soaked sheets and throw them in the laundry basket before stretching clean, dry sheets in their place. Then I step into the shower and wash away the perspiration of fear and loss. Doing this keeps my mind occupied but the warm water in the small, freezing bathroom cannot wash away the sadness that envelops me. And afterwards there come the anger and the other questions.

Who keeps their word?

Even my brother disappeared after the Captain's death. Yes, I went before him but I kept in touch, by letter and by telephone, whereas he seemed simply to disappear from the face of the earth.

Who considers another more than they consider themselves?

If my love for Nikolai were unadulterated, would I still be here, alive and healthy and working, as his skin and flesh and

116

eyes and hair turn to whatever it is they become before turning into dust.

In the face of failure, our lives are a lie and the lie becomes a road to nowhere. There is a moment when summer turns to autumn and a moment when autumn turns to winter, but we can never identify that moment. All we can do is recognise it after it has happened.

Once, when we were camping in the desert, I heard someone singing a song around the campfire and one of the lines lodged in my head: 'It's just that I thought a lover had to be some kind of liar too.' It's one of the few maxims I have remembered from that time.

'Gentlemen,' I say and the choristers fall silent, 'before you go home, I want you write down some words.'

The students fumble in their bags, producing pens, pencils, notebooks, tattered sheets of paper.

'We're ready, sir,' one of them says. 'Except Popov.'

'I'm ready, sir,' Popov says earnestly.

'Write this, please: "The angel said: Don't be afraid, Mary, for you have found favour with God."'

Bent heads, pens and pencils moving and then a hesitation as they wait for more.

'Is that it, sir?'

'That's it.'

'And what are we to do with it?'

'You could think about it.'

'Not a lot to think about, sir,' Popov says. 'In fact I've thought about it.'

The others laugh.

'And the conclusion you've come to?'

'It's from the Bible,' he says.

There's further laughter and cries of: 'Brilliant.' 'Popov the genius.'

'Wow, did you work that out yourself, Valentin?'

The uproar seems to frighten Popov. He is afraid that I'll blame him for the din.

'I'm not being funny, sir. It's just that I'm not sure what we're supposed to get from it. That's all.'

He looks about him, willing the other boys to be silent.

'You've probably got all you'll get from it – ever,' someone sniggers.

He blushes.

'It's all right,' I say quietly and I wait for the clamour to die down.

'It is, Valentin, as you say, from the Bible, from Luke's gospel, to be precise: the annunciation.'

'I knew that, sir,' Popov says, too quickly.

'Yeah, you did! We believe you,' the voice comes clearly, sarcastically from the back of the room.

I wait, again, for silence and, finally, it falls.

'All I want is that you think about those words and I want you to listen to this.'

Reaching behind me, I press Play on the CD player and the music begins, Mussorgsky's 'The Angel Said'.

The students listen, enthralled, their faces beaming, already mouthing the unfamiliar tune, listening for the words, wanting to sing. And then the music ends.

'Tomorrow we'll begin work on that piece. In the meantime, think about those words.'

Notebooks and pens are put away, satchels are thrown over shoulders and the students begin to shuffle out.

Popov stands at my desk.

'Sir.'

'Yes, Valentin?'

'I wasn't being smart with you, sir, about the sentence you gave us to write.'

'I know that,' I say, smiling. 'It's not a problem.'

'Good,' he says but he doesn't leave.

'Is there something else, Valentin?'

'Yes, sir, but I don't know if it's something I should say to you. It's difficult, but I need to talk to someone about it.'

I look into his face, the stern face of a nineteen-year-old who is still at sea in the world.

'Would you like to come for a cup of coffee?' I ask. 'We could walk to the Chay restaurant. If you like, but only if it suits you to talk today.'

'It suits me, sir, if you have the time.'

Popov packs his bag and I gather my bits and pieces and we walk together to the tearoom on the corner of the street, music huffing from the shadow of a doorway.

'One thing,' I say, as we sit down. 'In here, you are Valentin and I'm Andrew. "Sir" stays outside with the accordion player.'

Popov winces and swallows.

'I'll try.'

I order two coffees and sour cherry vareniki.

'So, are you enjoying the music?' I ask.

He nods.

'Actually, let me withdraw that question. Let's leave "sir" and "music school" outside the door and enjoy our food without giving academia a thought.'

He smiles and I'm reminded, for a moment, of the shadowed smile of the man I once knew, the young man dismounting from horseback, elated but cautious about sharing his elation.

The waitress arrives and the coffee and cakes are served.

'Eat up,' I say. 'These are most definitely not going back to the kitchen!'

Valentin and I eat and drink and make small talk about the goings on in the city.

'It is okay for me to say something to you that may surprise you?' he asks.

'Of course.'

'And....'

He sputters, a crumb of vareniki catching in his throat, so I pick up his sentence. 'And you can be assured of my discretion. What we speak of here remains here and if we speak of it again, then that will be all right, too. This conversation will have no bearing on anything that happens in the choir.'

He nods and breathes deeply, staring at his cup, uncertain, uneasy.

'We'll have more coffee,' I say, signalling the waitress.

While we wait, I listen to the music coming from the street. The wheezing of the accordion reminds me of my own harmonica playing from twenty years before.

'I played the harmonica,' I say quietly.

Popov looks up.

'Did you, sir? I can't imagine that.'

'Ah, we all have skeletons in the cupboard. My brother liked me to play it while he worked in the evenings.'

'You have a brother, sir?'

'Yes,' I say with more certainty than I feel. 'Just the one.'

'Does he teach music, sir?'

I let the formality go, knowing how hard it is to break a habit.

'No, he builds boats.'

'That's different. From teaching music I mean. Chalk and cheese.'

'Yes.'

The waitress arrives with the fresh coffees.

'It's about Nikolai Kalinnikov,' Popov says quickly, once she has left.

'Really?'

'Yes, sir.'

'His death was such a waste of talent...of life,' I say. 'He was a bright young man.'

'And great fun.' Valentin's eyes are suddenly bright and more alive than I've seen them before. 'I was in love with him.'

I say nothing, not because I'm surprised or hurt but because I'm thinking of Nikolai, remembering his smile and his hair tossing as he hurried along the corridor or crossed the street.

'I've shocked you, sir.'

'Good heavens no, not at all. It's just that I was thinking of his hair, how beautiful it looked, even in death. It was still bright and full of life. I identified him at the morgue and I remember how vibrant his hair seemed. His skin was blue and lifeless, but his hair still looked as though it was waiting for him to get up and run so that it could lift in the breeze. I know that sounds strange but it's true.'

Popov shakes his head and there is a film of tears about to shatter in his eyes.

'I'm sorry,' I say. 'I'm talking too much. I came here to listen.'

'No, sir, it's wonderful to talk about Nikolai. Some of the other fellows talk about him now and then, but almost as though they're afraid, as though his death might be contagious. Some just want to forget the accident ever happened but that means forgetting him, denying his existence.'

'You two were close. I hadn't known.'

'Not in choir. We were careful not to be too close in choir – people talk and snigger. We didn't want that.'

'I understand.'

'Every day I pass his photograph in the corridor and every day I think about him, sir, and I don't just miss him as a friend. I loved him. I loved the way he kissed me. I loved touching him. Does this make any sense, sir?'

'It does,' I say, thinking again of the young man on horseback but thinking, too, of Nikolai.

'He liked you, sir. Not that we don't all like you, but he talked a lot about you.'

'I'm glad to hear that.'

I can feel my own eyes filling, so I drink deeply, the bitter coffee cauterising my senses.

'How do I go on, sir? Does it get any better or does the pain ever get any duller, or do I give up?'

'I haven't seen my brother in almost twenty years,' I say. 'I have no idea if he's alive or dead, but I can't give up. I need to go on believing that I'll see him again.'

'I thought it would be easier, sir, by now. I thought things would have become more bearable but they just seem to be getting worse.'

'I don't believe, if you truly love someone, that their loss ever becomes bearable. You learn to accommodate the pain; I think that's as much as you should expect.'

And then we are silent and each of us in turn sips his coffee, an excuse for avoiding speech, and the music outside stops and, a few moments later, I see the accordion player pass the window of the coffee shop.

'I'm sorry for taking so much of your time, sir. I needed to tell someone. I don't know what else to say but I'd like if we could talk again, if you didn't mind, sir.'

'Nothing at all to be sorry about, Valentin. Of course we'll talk again. I'd like that. Nikolai was a fortunate young man and so are you – you had each other and you will always have each other.'

'Thank you,' he says. 'Thank you.'

Outside, darkness has descended. We walk to the street corner without speaking and stand at the spot where Nikolai died.

'Will you pray for me, sir?' Popov whispers.

'I think they shovel my prayers into the bottom of a bucket with the ash from hell,' I say.

He laughs.

The tram rail hums at our feet. We walk together to the tram stop.

'Thank you for the coffee and cakes,' Popov says.

'You're most welcome.'

A tram judders into sight and eventually squeals to a halt beside us.

'This is mine,' he says.

'Safe travelling. And we'll talk again about Nikolai, about anything. Nothing will ever change what was between you. That's a wonderful thing. Love is never truly lost,' I say.

He smiles gently and I can understand what Nikolai saw in him. And then he's gone and I turn and trudge slowly back towards my flat, avoiding the cemetery, taking the longer way through the evening streets, remembering the sound of harmonica music from long ago. And I think of Valentin and Nikolai and I know that soon it will be time for me to think about going home to the warmth of the summer sand.

Buying and Selling

Was that precisely what he'd said? Thaddeus wondered. He'd said so many things over the years they'd travelled together, that much of it was becoming a confusion.

Sometimes, Thaddeus read the books that had been written about those years and the man and the philosophy and he wondered where the journalists and biographers and critics were coming from, where they'd unearthed their so-called information, how they'd reached the conclusions they had. Very little of what he read bore any resemblance to the things he remembered. He didn't remember there ever being a philosophy as such. Ways of doing things had emerged over the weeks and months; they had learned from experience and often the suggestions had come from one or other of the group members but, by no stretch of the imagination, would Thaddeus call it a philosophy.

Could two and a half decades have bewildered his memory to that extent? He doubted it. He didn't forget important things. He could walk into his office now and lay his hand on the exact key to any of the forty cars in the sales yard without even checking the registration numbers on the plastic ties. And he still had an eagle eye for the occasional opportunity, but the opportunities were becoming fewer and farther between. That's why there were forty cars in the yard. He'd never had this many before, even in the eighties, never been caught carrying so much immovable stock.

It's not what you achieve but what you believe.

Yes, that was what he'd said. Not at one of the rallies but over a meal on a summer night. Afterwards, Thaddeus and Al had stayed on for a last, late drink. Al was flying off somewhere the next morning, off in search of another story that might make a book. Those were the days before any of Al's books had seen the light of day. Thaddeus had admired the younger man's energy but doubted his story-chasing would ever amount to anything. Ideas were one thing but opportunities to change the world were the real thing.

'Sounds like he's getting us ready for a change,' Al had said.

'In what way?'

'Don't know. Just does. He talked about belief not achievement. There's a difference.'

'Believe to achieve,' Thaddeus laughed. 'It's a good motto.'

'Is it? Seems to me it's just a motto and, anyway, that's not what he's saying.'

Thaddeus remembered shrugging.

'You're over-analysing, man. You read too much. Stay rooted.'

'Maybe.'

'For sure. We're on the right track here. You should stick around.'

'I'll be back in a couple of weeks.'

'The books can wait.'

'I don't know if they can,' Al had said. 'But I'll get there, wherever there is. Maybe that's the problem with me: I don't really know where there is.'

Looking back, Thaddeus remembers his young friend as a man waiting for magic to find him, believing in the sunlight, filled with a genuine expectation that someone would come, a white witch, a wizard casting a spell, bringing him the gifts of joy and certainty, offerings in which he hardly dared believe.

And then he looks at himself. A man standing on a garage forecourt, stock list in hand, amid all the shining, unsold second-hand cars. Not that they're advertised as such. They're 'pre-owned' now, as though Thaddeus has been keeping them warm, running them in for whichever lucky punter walks through the gate on this spring afternoon.

His dog ambles from behind one of the cars and comes to him. Together they sit on the office step, the soft sunlight painting their bodies. Thaddeus leaves the stock list on the concrete tread and rubs the dog's warm coat and then his ears until the animal moans softly, singing a song of pleasure and companionship.

'We all have stories and reasons not to tell them,' Thaddeus says out loud and the dog looks up at him, listening for familiar words like walk or dinner, but they don't come.

Thaddeus rubs the dog's ears again and lowers his own head, sinking his face into the dog's coat, breathing the smell of animal life and freedom, each deeply drawn breath a point of recollection and reconciliation. He is aware of two hearts beating, his own and the dog's. He listens, trying to match the rhythms to each other but the patterns are not the same. One is uncertain, more an erratic throb than a beat, the other is calm and measured, loyal and trusting.

He especially loves the smell of the dog's coat, drying in the sunshine after rain. That deep, dark smell drawn from a thousand unknown scents, that smell which catches some inkling of the depths of senses we will never know.

A shadow falls across his face and he looks up.

A young woman is standing in front of him, her features masked by the aura of sunlight about her.

'You sell cars?' she asks.

'Yes. I certainly do.'

'I'd like to look at one or two.'

'Of course.'

He stands up, shielding his eyes.

'I like your dog,' she says.

'He's not for sale,' Thaddeus laughs.

'I would hope not.'

They walk across the sales yard.

'What did you have in mind? Cheap and cheerful or something more solid.'

'I'm not sure. Let's look.'

He walks and talks her through the lines of cars. He's in no rush; there's no one else about, he has all afternoon and so, it seems, does she. He explains the benefits of one car above another, checking prices against his stock list as if he didn't already know the cost of every car and the amount by which he is prepared to reduce it. And each time he mentions a lower figure, she moves to the next vehicle and asks about colours or upholstery or wheel trims.

'You're not here to buy a car, are you?' Thaddeus asks finally.

'No.' Her reply is definite.

'Just passing an afternoon?'

'No. I wanted to talk to you.'

'About?'

'Him. Then. About what really happened.'

'I don't talk about him or then. And everybody knows what happened.'

'Bullshit,' the young woman says. 'Those who don't really care assume they know; those who care realise they don't know.'

'And you care?'

'That's why I'm here.'

'Oh come on,' Thaddeus barks a sharp cackle. 'You're here for a story. You're a journalist. You smell a story, an old one but a story nevertheless.'

'Is that a crime?'

'Not at all and I wish you well with it. It's just that the story isn't here.'

'I'd write it sympathetically.'

'I have no doubt but that you would,' he says sarcastically.

'You don't believe me?'

'Belief doesn't come into it. There is no story here. Trust me. Not the one you're looking for; I don't think it exists. It's a figment of your editor's imagination. Let me guess. He's in his fifties, one-time student activist, imagines himself a freethinker. He's a conservative dressed in liberal clothing, trying to get you to recreate some element of the dream he thinks he missed out on. You do realise that sending you here is that middle-aged man's surrogate fantasy.'

'You've thought about all this.'

'You're not the first journalist to come around here. Some of them bring money, some come in short skirts, some are aggressive, some have that extra button open on their blouses – I've seen all the tacks they take. Sorry, that *you* take, trust me.'

'Trust doesn't come into it.' The young woman smiles. 'Believe me. There is a story.'

'Well, if there is, it's not here,' Thaddeus says again.

'How's business?'

'Fantastic! You're the millionth customer we've had this month. That's something about which I'll happily give you a story – cars that won't sell, I can ladle out heart-breaking stuff about a staff of four reduced to one. I can even give you an idea for a headline. The soundless silence. And the first line, if you want. Forty gleaming, driverless cars form a silent traffic jam, an image of the new republic. See, I've done half the work for you already. Or I can give you an angle. Look, down there, seven four-wheel drives, not one of them more than two years old, each of them an aspiration that crashed in metaphorical flames. Actually, maybe that's not a good analogy. Each a dream that withered on the vine of illusory success.'

The young woman laughs.

'You're impressed, I can see,' Thaddeus smiles. 'In return for your listening, you get a free key ring.'

Rummaging in his jacket pocket, he produces a fob and hands it to the woman.

'Thank you,' she says. 'But you don't like me, do you?'

'Actually I do.'

She seems surprised.

'I don't like what you're doing or how you tried to do it but I do like you. Something you said.'

'What did I say?'

'You said "I would hope not" about my dog not being for sale.'

She nods.

'You can have a cup of coffee if you want,' Thaddeus says. 'But no story.'

The woman nods again and they walk towards the office. Thaddeus draws up a chair and motions her to sit down. The dog settles at her feet. Thaddeus pours two coffees, clears a space on his desk, pushes sachets of milk and sugar towards the young woman, takes a packet of biscuits from a drawer and sits opposite her.

The woman sips her coffee.

'What was he like?' she asks, as nonchalantly as though she were asking about a set of seat covers.

Thaddeus allows himself a smile and a raised eyebrow but says nothing.

'It's just a story at this stage,' the woman says.

'Then you could make it up, give your imagined version. Others have.'

'That's not how I work.'

'Good for you.'

Thaddeus stares through the plateglass window that frames five miles of countryside. Across the distant fields, the haze gives way to memory. He looks back through the mists of spring to an evening long ago and sees his father in a garden.

'I'll tell you a story,' he says.

The woman looks up but doesn't reach for her recorder.

'It had been raining all that afternoon,' Thaddeus says quietly. 'But the late light and the evening breeze were sucking the dampness out of the raised drills. My father bent and dug out one last sod near the headland of the garden. "Now," he called. Called to me. "Bring him out." I was a young boy then, ten or eleven, used to doing as I was told, but I hesitated. "Bring him on," my father said again. "The sooner we get this done, the better; you're only prolonging his misery."

'I turned and opened a shed door. From the darkness, an old dog hobbled into the garden. It seemed to me that it was suddenly twilight and that the warmth had gone out of the sun.

'"Bring him over," my father called. "It'll save us carrying him."

'I put my hand on the dog's shoulder and he looked up at me.

'"Come on," I said quietly. I was hoping the dog wouldn't hear or would disobey but, instead, he wagged his tired tail, his eyes brightened momentarily and he struggled in my wake, along the narrow path to where my father stood, crowbar in hand.

'"See," my father said. "He can hardly walk. We're doing him the best turn anyone ever done him."

'The dog didn't look up to the place from which my father's voice had come. Instead he held my gaze, I know it was because he trusted me. The breeze was lifting his long coat and then it seemed to me that his head exploded. My father had brought the crowbar down heavily, the point crashed through the dog's skull. For a moment, the animal went on embracing me with that unquestioning look and his eyes filled up with blood and slowly they begin to drip, then gush. Blood was bulging from his sockets and suddenly it spouted out. And, just as abruptly, the dog's legs buckled and he fell on his side, away from the open grave. There was no sound. I had heard nothing, no splitting skull, no breaking bone, no whimper, no bark.

'My father put his boot on the animal's side, jerking the crowbar from his skull.

'"Never felt it," he said.

'I was mesmerised by the tears of blood drip, drip, dripping on the evening clay. My father heaved the dog's carcass with the toe of his boot and rolled it awkwardly into the hole he had dug. There was nothing left only the dark blots of drying blood on the clay.'

The young woman is silent.

'There's your story,' Thaddeus says quietly.

'Thank you.'

For a long time they sit in silence. Finally, the young woman takes her bag from the floor and stands up.

'Thank you again.'

Thaddeus drains his coffee cup and walks her to the door.

'I hope I didn't waste your afternoon,' she says.

'Millionth customer, glad to see you,' he smiles. 'You've got your free key ring?'

She opens her palm; the key ring rests in it.

'You should have been a writer,' she says.

'No, that was someone else's job, but we won't go there. And now it's your job. Good luck with it.'

Bending, the young woman pats the dog, then walks towards the road.

'If you know of anyone looking for a good car, tell them about us,' Thaddeus calls after her.

The woman waves without turning and disappears around the yard gate. Thaddeus sits again on the office step and buries his face in the warm hair of this dog, the dog whose smell reminds him of the smell of that other dog on long ago, faraway shining days. And he thinks of a summer evening after rain in another garden. He's there with a girl, dark-haired, like the young woman who has just left. The girl is saying, 'It's the most beautiful evening of my life.' They're standing in the shadow of a tree and an hour has passed since she agreed to marry him.

As they watch, a dunnock flies into the paws of a skulking cat and from there into the cat's jaws. He wonders what the dunnock was thinking to be so easily caught. Was it thinking only of food or was it not thinking at all? Was it celebrating the summer day that was ending, yet another summer day on top of all the other summer days stretching back across the weeks?

'It seemed to be filled with joy when it flew into the cat's paws, the cat's claws, the cat's jaws,' Thaddeus says. 'It was singing.'

'Birds are addicted to singing,' she says. 'It's not a conscious choice. It is an addiction.'

And he knows, in that instant, that they will never marry.

Even now, thirty-five years later, sitting on the sunlit step of this failing second-hand car business, he has no idea how or why he knew, intuitively, that what had just been agreed would never happen. He has never been able to fathom why, suddenly, they were losing one another, why something in her tone told him everything he didn't want to know.

'Gardens are not always good places,' Thaddeus says.

The dog looks up at him, then rolls on its back, wanting its belly rubbed.

Thaddeus obliges, laughing as he does so.

Absent Children

I moved away from the river when its invitation became too strong. Ironically, that growing temptation coincided with the arrival of summer. All winter I had lived on the banks of the cold, fast torrent without once sensing that its drab and dreary arms might appeal to me. But the arrival of the warmer days and the turning of the water from grey to blue brought a growing fascination that terrified me.

So I packed up and left, driving across country, moving along narrow roads that twisted, or so my map informed me, farther and farther from any significant body of water. When, eventually, I stopped in some two-horse town, my pick-up wouldn't start and the local mechanic was less than optimistic about it ever starting again.

'It might but you'll have to talk nicely to it.'

'How nicely?'

'Hundreds.'

'How many?'

'Six or seven – new engine at least. Maybe more, maybe eight or nine.'

'Right.'

'But you don't have it?'

I shook my head.

'Looks like I'll have to consider the possibility of work,' I said.

'Does that scare you?'

'Not at all. I just hadn't planned on staying anywhere so soon.'

'And definitely not here?'

I looked down the long, empty street framed between a pair of ancient gas pumps, pursed my lips and smiled.

'You don't need to say no more than's been said,' the mechanic grunted. 'If I could get you going, I would, but this lady won't be persuaded.'

He patted the roof of the pick-up. There was something in his tone that made me believe he wasn't trying to make an easy buck.

'I understand,' I said.

He looked me in the eye for twenty or thirty seconds, a long time.

'My brother has work that needs doing; been under some pressure lately,' he said quietly.

'What kind of work?'

'Farm work, tractor stuff. If you can nurse this thing along, then you could drive a tractor. He has timber that needs drawing, hedges that need cutting – nothing too complicated.'

'I could do that.'

'I'll call him.'

The mechanic's brother lived at the end of a long lane in a large, squat house that had a porch that ran around all four sides. It stood on the edge of a pinewood, resting on the top of a hill and eyeing an enormous cornfield that ran away in three directions, for ever it seemed.

His barn and machinery sheds were on the other side of the wood so that, approaching the house along the lane, as we did in the mechanic's car, there was no hint that this was a farmhouse. Instead, the building looked like it had sprouted from the trees, finding its own form and making itself available to the humans who had, eventually, found themselves beneath its roof.

The mechanic dropped me at the garden gate and waved me away.

'They'll be inside; they're expecting you. I'll call you about the pick-up.'

'No hurry,' I said. 'I won't be able to pay you for at least a couple of weeks.'

He shrugged.

'If I get it going you can drive and pay later.'

'I might do a runner.'

He shrugged again.

'I don't think you're the kinda fella that would.'

And he was gone, the wheels mounting the low bank near the gateway as he turned his car.

I lifted the latch on the garden gate and stepped into a patch of ground that might once have been a garden. It still had the contours of a garden – with the outlines of paths and beds – and there were straggling pockets of flowers, beaten flat by the weight of incessant sunlight, but nothing had been sown there in years.

The dominant smell was of stock. Night was falling fast and the air was suddenly thick with its scent. I had always imagined the scent of stock to be red and blue and I tried to visualise those colours as I climbed the six steps that took me onto the wooden porch of the unlit house. There was no sound – no radio or TV playing, no dogs barking, none of the noises that I'd have expected from a lived-in house.

For a moment a series of awful thoughts crossed my mind. The mechanic had dropped me here knowing the place was empty. My pick-up was already on the back of a low-loader, heading for a scrapyard. The guy didn't even own the garage in which I'd met him. This was all a swizz and by the time I walked or hitched back to town, I'd be too late to do anything about it.

'You the fella looking for work?'

The voice was gloomy and came from a dim, deep doorway. Peering into the twilight, I could just make out a figure in what seemed like a hallway and then a light was suddenly switched on and a middle-aged man towered above me, backlit, his features shadowed.

'You the fella?' he asked again.

'Yes. Philip.'

'Jake.'

I offered my hand but it was left unshaken.

'My brother dropped ya?'

'Yes.'

Jake stood aside and I stepped into the long hallway.

'Nice smell of stock out there,' I said.

He didn't answer. Instead, I was ushered along the hall and through a doorway into a large room. The man flicked the light switch as we passed from one room to the other and I found myself in an enormous kitchen. He indicated a chair at the rambling table and I sat there.

'You want coffee?'

'That'd be nice.'

'You eaten?'

I shook my head.

'There's something we had for dinner. I'll heat it up.'

'Thank you.'

A gas ring went click click click and then spurted into life.

'You drive a tractor?'

'Yes.'

'Combine?'

'Yes.'

'Okay. I got maybe twelve weeks' work here. You on for that?'

'Yes. My pick-up is kaput. Your brother is going to fix it.'

'He said.'

'Yes.'

A spoon rattled in a saucepan and a plate was taken from a cupboard.

'You have a fine place here.'

'Six-hundred acres.'

'Nice.'

'Work.'

'Course.'

'Just work.'

The spoon rattled again, followed by the sound of food slopping onto a plate and then a rattling in a cutlery drawer.

'You wanna beer?'

'No thanks.'

The plate arrived, piled high with stew. A knife, fork and spoon were laid beside it.

'Bread?'

'No, this is great. Thanks.'

I ate. The food was tasty.

'You make this yourself? It's really good.'

'No.'

I ate some more and the man sat opposite me.

'Have you been farming here a long time?'

'Long enough.'

I nodded and went back to my food. The man was silent, watching me eat. When I'd finished, he took the plate and cutlery away and led me out, across a small yard, to a low building.

Inside, there were four sets of bunks.

'Take your pick,' he said. 'Blankets and the like in the cupboard over there; shower and the rest through there. Breakfast at seven.'

And then he was gone, the door closing quietly behind him, leaving me in the sparse bunkhouse that seemed, suddenly, full of the ghosts of long-lost cowboys.

I woke before six the following morning, showered and then loafed around the bunkhouse for half an hour before tapping on the kitchen door and stepping inside.

A slight, fair-haired woman was standing at the stove, her back to me.

'Good morning,' I said.

'Good morning,' she said quietly, turning and smiling. She was in her forties, I guessed. Her face was pale and drawn, her eyes a dull, dead blue.

'I'm Philip,' I said.

'Emily.'

Her husband lumbered into the room and nodded towards me. We sat at the kitchen table, eating for the most part in silence. Whatever conversation happened revolved around farm work. Jake seemed anxious to assure himself that I could do what needed doing.

'Don't need a sidekick,' he said. 'Gotta work on your own.'

'I can do that.'

'Good.'

I did work on my own and day by day, week after week, through that first month, Jake came to trust me. In the beginning, there were tasks he set for me and then checked. Then there were tasks that were set, with which I was entrusted, and, by the end of that month, I was allowed to get on with the work that I thought needed doing.

In the third week, my pick-up was returned and I paid a quarter of what I owed Jake's brother.

While the summer unbolted its door, my evenings were occasionally filled with work but sometimes offered freedom. When that happened, I drove into town, caught a movie, drank a few beers and came back to the farm.

One evening, as I pulled into the yard, I saw Emily sitting on the porch, a book in her hand. I parked the pick-up and went and sat on the step below her. By then, the book had disappeared.

'That your garden?' I asked, nodding at the ragged collection of overgrown colour.

'It was.'

'I could do something with it, if you want. Dig it over, weed it.'

She shivered and shook her head.

'Well, if you change your mind. I have time on my hands.'

The evening sun rinsed the enormous wheat fields in a profound, rich gold and the sky deepened from a light to a darker blue.

'Enough to look after.'

'Okay. But the offer stands.'

'Thank you.'

Sometimes we ate together in silence. In the first few weeks, I'd try to make conversation but it seemed like a pointless exercise, so I stepped into the silence that was Jake and Emily's natural habitat, accepting what I couldn't change. Some days we met for breakfast, lunch and dinner and never spoke at all and, when we did, I found myself drawn into the disconnected monosyllables that passed for conversation or didn't. I could never decide whether they despised or delighted in their lake of silence.

Nothing in their eyes or mouths gave any inkling, nothing in their physicality betrayed love or hate or like or boredom. Emily's eyes remained the same lacklustre blue, picking nothing of the summer light from the sky. Jake's taciturnity bordered on the obsessive. He behaved as if a word would shatter whatever it was that held his world together. He never looked me in the eye, not even for a moment. Instead, his eyes constantly ploughed the ground around him, afraid the earth might dissipate or disappear if it slipped out of his sight. Even when he drove the tractor, he never seemed to trust the horizon. His gaze fell ten feet ahead of the front wheels, constantly checking that the world was not flat, that it wouldn't suddenly reach a precipice and slip from beneath him, sending him tumbling into nothingness.

One Sunday afternoon, as I was turning the pick-up in the yard, I saw Emily take her place on the porch, book in hand. Slowing, I leaned through the open window and shouted across.

'Do you want me to bring you a book from town?'

'What?' She frowned.

'A book. You must be close to finishing that one.'

'I don't read books,' she said, pushing the book behind her.

'Okay,' I said. 'Anything you want? Provisions? Anything?'

She shook her head.

'You want to come for the ride? Won't be too long.'

Another shake of the head.

'Okay,' I said again, but not so she could hear.

One morning after breakfast, when Jake had gone out to check the wheat for cutting, I went back into the kitchen to get my hat. Emily was sitting at the table, her back to me, her book lying open on the scrubbed wooden boards.

Passing the table, I saw, before she had time to close it, that the pages of the journal were covered in neat, copperplate handwriting, the lines indented, numbers and words like mathematic poems.

She blushed – the first colour I'd seen in her face – and swept the book into her lap, closing it as she did.

'I wasn't trying to read it,' I said.

'No.'

'Just came back for my hat.'

'Yes.'

'It's burning up out there, even this early.'

'Yes.'

'I thought you heard me come in.'

She smiled a half-smile and then quickly looked away.

I took my hat from the chair and angled it onto my head.

'I'm sorry,' I said. 'I hope you believe me.'

'I do.'

'That's good. I wouldn't want you thinking otherwise.'

It was two or three evenings later. I was washing the cab of the pick-up when Emily came down the yard.

'There's some coffee inside, fresh brewed,' she said.

I had never been invited into the house in the eight weeks I'd been there, other than to eat, never spoken to her other than out of necessity, never encouraged to believe there might even be a cause for conversation, so I didn't move. As far as I was concerned, she was, for reasons best known to herself, imparting this information. I had no cause to believe this was an invitation.

Halfway back to the house, she seemed to realise I wasn't following, so she stopped and turned.

'There's apple and cinnamon pie too.'

Her soft voice carried in the still evening air.

'You mean for me to come in?'

'If you want.'

'Thank you,' I said, dropping the sponge back into the wash pail.

Inside, the kitchen smelled like one of those patisseries that draw you in and won't let you out. I closed my eyes and breathed deeply.

'Reminds me of the bakeries in Paris,' I said, but there was no response.

On the kitchen table a pie bulged and puffed, cinnamon steaming off its pastried back.

'Sit,' she said and I did.

She brought coffee, cream, sugar and plates to the table and then went back to get knives and forks.

'Can I help?'

'All done,' she said, sitting across from me.

'Jake not joining us?'

'He's gone to town. Needs something from his brother for the combine. Reckons the time is just about right.'

'Could be,' I said. 'Don't think that wheat will get much riper.'

She sliced the pie and a gust of steam rose and hung a moment above the table, pastry wrapping itself around the steaming fruit, the fragrance of cinnamon stronger now, catching the nose and resting on the tongue.

'You can taste cinnamon before you taste it,' I said. 'One of those smells that lands in your mouth like a…butterfly.'

She laughed, the first time I'd ever seen her laugh, but her eyes were still indifferent and flat.

'I hope this don't taste like butterfly,' she said.

'I have no doubt it won't.'

She lifted the coffee pot and poured, first for me, then for herself.

I lifted a forkful of pie and held it beneath my nose, relishing the scents, allowing the fruit to cool, anticipating.

She watched as I slipped the pie between my lips, waited for me to taste and smile and chew and swallow. Only then did she lift her fork and break a morsel from the slice on her own plate.

We ate and drank in silence and the sun sank lower, its light stretching and lengthening the shadows of the window frames across the kitchen floor, catching the side of Emily's face and her hair.

I wanted to say something, to tell her what I was seeing, but I didn't dare.

'This pie is indescribable,' I said. 'Best I've ever eaten. Hey, I'm not even eating it; it's melting in my mouth.'

She smiled her half-smile again.

'You want some more?'

'What about Jake?'

'Don't eat it.'

'Well, then I will.'

She cut another slice and poured more coffee and then she took her book from somewhere down the side of her chair and placed it on the table, pushing it gently, fractionally towards me.

'That's it,' she said. 'All in there.'

'May I read?'

She nodded.

I reached across, lifted the hard-backed journal and pushed my plate to one side. I opened the book and found myself reading a recipe for bread. Overleaf, there was one for asparagus soup and then one for a beef stew and another for chocolate cake and so the recipes went on, page after page after page, the book bulging with neat, well-thumbed pages of good food.

'Your life's work?' I asked.

'Seven years,' she said.

'You ought to try to get these printed – sell copies in town.'

She laughed again, a hard and charmless laugh that was at odds with the care that had gone into the book I was holding.

'Where's the recipe for that apple pie?'

She reached across and flicked some pages, her hand brushing mine.

'There,' she said and I read the words that described what I'd just smelled, tasted and eaten. Words shaped with care, as if they were a poem or a song or something, like they were meant to be enjoyed for themselves, never mind what they were describing.

'You write a lovely hand.'

'Thank you.'

'And bake angelic fare.'

'It's just a pie.'

'What I buy in the store is just a pie. This is the reason Eve got kicked out of Eden. And I'm glad she did.'

She arched her hands beneath her chin, nodded and looked at the remnants in the pie dish. I leafed through another few pages but I wanted to talk, I didn't want to read.

'How many recipes?'

'About six hundred.'

'You've got to do something with those.'

'I don't think so. I dream 'em up, sometimes I make 'em and then I write 'em in this book. That's enough. That's it.'

We sat in silence and the sunlight retreated through the windowpanes and then Emily stood up, turned on the lights and began clearing the dishes.

'Let me help,' I said.

'No, you go. Jake'll be home soon. It's getting late.'

'Thank you again,' I said.

'It was an apple pie, that's all.'

'For letting me read your book.'

'Just recipes.'

I knew she didn't mean that, but I said nothing more.

A couple of days later, Jake was out in the barn – I could hear the combine engine turning over – and I came up to the yard to collect a tool box.

Emily was sitting on the porch again, her book on her lap, head bent, but she was crying. From twenty yards I could see her tears when the sunlight caught them, thin little rainbows slipping from under her hair.

I crossed the yard and stood at the foot of the porch steps.

'You okay?'

She looked up. Her eyes were red nicks, like wounds that might never heal.

'Can I do anything to help?'

Her head turned slowly from side to side, as though she hardly had the energy to move it.

'Just say if there is,' I said.

She stared but I knew she was neither seeing nor hearing me, so I backed away, picked up the toolbox from inside the shed doorway and followed the cranky sound of the combine, back to work.

That night, after dinner, while Jake was outside checking the night sky for weather, I asked again if she was all right.

'Not sleeping is all,' she said.

'Awake all night?'

'I sleep at dawn. Dawn is whenever tiredness comes.'

'That's a nice way of putting it.'

'Is it?'

'Yes it is.'

The kitchen door opened and Jake blustered in.

'Start cutting tomorrow,' he said.

I nodded.

'Weather's gonna hold. Gonna call Timber, get him to organise the trailers. You and me, we'll do the combining in shifts. Twelve on, twelve off.'

And that's how it was, Jake and me in turns in the cab of the combine. He worked days and I worked nights, the big sallow moon sitting above the enormous, uncluttered cornfields. The tractors and trailers beside me in the darkness, the cab a glass box filled with music or simply with the familiar throbbing of the perpetual engine noises, the hum and whine; the saw and grind; the tension and release, hour by twilit hour through the half-dark night. Sometimes swinging the cabin door open to let the tractor noises and the cooler air of night come in.

Sometimes lost in the songs from the radio. Sometimes beguiled by the sinking moon or the blush of dawn. Sometimes fighting sleep by shouting and laughing to myself. Sometimes stopping and climbing down to share a coffee and smoke a cigarette with a tractor driver before we both returned to the work that waited impatiently for us.

And sometimes I imagined how that work might look from space, two machines, their headlights furrowing the earth before them, travelling slowly but methodically across the vast spaces of these malformed fields that had once been buffalo prairies. The viewer would see a pair of toy machines, driven by two lunatics whose waking and sleeping vision was riven by relentless lines of high, dry wheat.

In the morning, just after seven, Jake's truck would come across the vast field like a sheepdog in search of lost sheep and I'd climb down and he'd climb up, without a word, and I'd drive his truck back to the yard, roll into bed and sleep until midday. I'd eat and afterwards I'd sleep or read until an early suppertime and then go back to work.

So it went on for three days: sleep and eat and work and sleep and eat and work. I dreamt of wheat fields and the rise and fall of certain sections of the land, the way a field would gradually tip the combine to one side without ever threatening to flip it.

On the afternoon of the third day, I went into the house to have my lunch. The kitchen was empty, so I poured coffee and took food from the stove. Emily's recipe book had been left on the table and, as I ate, I casually opened and flicked quickly through it. There were pages marked with pieces of paper and newspaper cuttings and a few photographs acted as bookmarks at the beginnings of sections, but I didn't believe it was my place to look at them or read the cuttings. Instead, I ran my eyes over the recipes: Watermelon Wine; Stuffed Peppers; Pasta Penne.

I poured more coffee and put the book on the table beside me. A moment later, Emily came downstairs and into the kitchen.

'You're awake,' she said quietly and then, seeing the recipe book beside me, her tone changed. 'Have you been looking in my book?'

'I've just been daydreaming about your recipe for strawberry jelly,' I laughed. 'I could taste it off the page.'

'You had no right,' she said sharply.

'I'm sorry.'

'No right whatsoever.'

'Are you annoyed?'

'Annoyed isn't the word I'd use.'

'Angry then?'

'Very, very, very angry.' She spoke slowly, calmly, emphasising each syllable of every word.

'Why?'

'Why?' Her laughter was cold and hurt. 'If you have to ask, then you have no idea about anything and it's not my place to explain. The fact that you even ask that question is an answer in itself.'

'Right.'

I waited for her to continue but instead she picked the book from the table, crossed to the armchair near the window and sat there, her back to me. I saw her open the book, watched her head drop, imagined her eyes welded to the lines before her. I might not even have been in the room, such was her concentration. I recognised that intensity of absorption from a couple of days earlier and felt compelled to try to undo whatever wrong I'd done.

'You don't want to talk about this?'

Her only response was the very definite turning of a page. Who would have thought a sheet of paper could cut like that.

'Who would have thought the old man to have had so much blood in him?' I said for no better reason than that it had come into my head, but, again, no response, neither a sigh nor a movement.

I walked into the garden and sat in the shade of a buddleia. Butterflies rose and then resettled above me. From where I sat, I could see her through the kitchen window. Another page turned and still no break in her concentration. I closed my eyes and listened for the distant wash of passing traffic. The waves of early afternoon noise rising and falling, like the waves on the shore of that other sea a long time ago.

It was late in the afternoon when I took a bicycle from the barn and cycled down the long lane to the road. Passing the house, I saw that the armchair by the kitchen window was empty and I was disappointed. I wanted to apologise, wanted to wave and cross to the window, ask if she would like to cycle or walk with me, or at least have her exchange some words that I might take as a token of forgiveness. I didn't want to be at war with her. But the chair was empty and the window looked in on a neat and vacant room.

Reaching the end of the laneway, I turned right, away from town, and cycled quickly along the dusty roadway. It was good to be out and moving. In the last few days I had fallen into a pattern of sleep and work, forgetting that I needed relaxation too. As I rode, I promised myself two things – I would get some exercise every day during harvest time and I would mend the fences I had broken with Emily. I didn't believe that what I'd done was very wrong – it hadn't been my intention to be intrusive – but she obviously did and that was reason enough to apologise again.

On a bend at the head of a steep hill, about two miles from the house, I saw a small burial ground at the foot of the incline, half-hidden by an overgrowth of saplings and brushwood which formed an uneasy support for a low picket fence that had seen better days. Here and there the fence had collapsed entirely but mostly it hung in the summer air, supported by a sapling or a rotting post at one end and a tangle of dogwood at the other.

As I gathered speed, flashing between the hedgerows, a cloth of butterflies rose in the breeze and my face was washed and dried in the noiseless, rising rainbow of dying wings. Faster and faster I went, the air flecked and dappled with the plumes of swirling colours, the butterflies tumbling and turning in their outrageous and beautiful dance of death. And then, at last, the road levelled out and the bicycle slowed, giving the butterflies time to open their curtain and let me safely through. The bicycle slowed and slowed, the sound of its spokes becoming more methodical, their click click click returning to a regular pattern as I pedalled the flat, dusty road, eventually falling silent when I came to a standstill outside the gate of the decrepit burial ground.

I didn't go inside. Instead, I lay on the dry, burnt grass by the roadside, my hat tipped over my eyes, the bicycle lying beside me, and listened to the hot, tired songs of resting birds. Everything, it seemed, had wound down into the pit of this late summer afternoon.

An hour later, as I made my way back to the farm, the hill road was petalled with dead and dying butterflies. They lay still or broken-backed, their wings waving goodbye to the gift of flight. I tried to weave a way between them but it was impossible; their slaughter would not be ignored, their colours already losing lustre in the dust of the lengthening shadows.

Life is short, I thought, and the very banality of the idea was, in itself, a moment of epiphany. I was determined that I wouldn't allow what had happened that morning to destroy the delicate but definite connection between Emily and myself.

Back at the farmhouse, her armchair was still empty. I returned the bicycle to the barn, knocked at the kitchen door and walked inside. The room was empty, as it had been when I'd arrived for lunch.

I made some coffee and a sandwich. In two hours I'd be back in the combine cab, the falling darkness stretching itself across the wheat fields. I was determined not to begin the night without speaking to Emily. And then I heard her in the hallway and I called her name.

She came into the kitchen and I asked if she'd like some coffee.

'Okay,' she said.

We sat across the table from each other and I told her about the butterflies. She winced.

'I wanted to say I'm really sorry about your book. I just took it up without thinking.'

She nodded.

'I didn't mean to intrude. I'd never do that. I'd never barge into your life. I like you too much to do something like that.'

'I won't sleep with you,' she said quietly.

'That wasn't my aim.'

'No. But it would be. In time.'

'Would it?'

'Yes.'

'And yours?'

'It might have been.'

'It honestly hadn't crossed my mind.'

She arched an eyebrow.

'I just wanted you to know.'

'Too late for all that.'

'Because I opened your book?'

She laughed.

'You really don't know much, do you?'

I drove the combine through the night, trying not to think about Emily. I ordered the figures in my head, worked out that I'd be ready to pay off Jake's brother when the harvesting was done and I'd have enough to get me through the winter if I was careful. I examined the possibilities of staying a little while longer, maybe seeing out the winter. That would depend on whether or not Jake had work for me. But it would also depend on whether or not I wanted to stay.

One good thing had come of all this – I'd almost forgotten the river and the river's call. I knew I would never live near water again. And then I stopped thinking. I don't like to think too much. Thinking leads to the past and the past is not a healthy place for me to travel. I need to live in the here and now. When my heart says go, it's time to go. Thinking about the future inevitably leads back because the future and the past are equally uncertain. So I concentrated on the job in hand, tried to estimate where I would be when the tractor driver next stopped for a break.

Every couple of hours we stopped for coffee and a cigarette and I and whichever one of Timber's men happened to be on the service tractor sat on the steps of the combine and shot the breeze. Sometimes we talked about movies or music or sport or the women in the town bar.

'You cutting any corn in there?'

I shook my head.

'Good-looking guy like you. I am surprised.'

'Nice of you to say so,' I laughed; 'nothing doing.'

'Women love that European accent, specially out here where they don't get much of anything they ain't got before, one way and another.'

He stubbed his cigarette carefully on the step, gargled a mouthful of coffee and spat it into the light from his tractor.

'I'm telling ya, you just talk low and slow and you'll have more pussy 'n you'd get in a cattery.'

'Sounds attractive.'

'Don't knock it, buddy; it's wet and it's willing,' he said, swinging down onto the stubbled earth. 'Guess we better get moving or Jake'll be saying we stole his time. I reckon that guy can hear in his sleep.'

'You think so?'

'See, that's just what I mean,' the driver laughed, pointing at me.

'You talk like that, low and slow, the way you said think so, to any woman in this town and the gates of Eden will spring open faster'n you can get your belt unbuckled.'

We finished the harvesting at the end of that week and, when I got my money from Jake, I drove into town and paid off what I owed on the pick-up. Driving back to the farm, I noticed a change in the evening, a subtle alteration in the sky, reminding me that the season was ending.

That night, over supper, I asked Jake if there was work enough for me to stay on for a couple of months.

'You want to?'

'If there's work.'

'Stay on a time. I'll tell you when the work runs out.'

And that was it.

We set about the ploughing. This was less frenetic than the harvesting. We worked a normal day and if something didn't get done, it could always get done the next day. A couple of times a week I'd go into town for a beer, meet one of two of Timber's tractor men, shoot some pool, chat to the girls in the bar. I took one of them out to dinner a couple of times and we caught a handful of movies, but that was it. Something might have happened but neither one of us ever seemed to want to take it beyond a goodnight kiss in my pick-up truck.

'We could go on like this,' she said one night. 'But that's just habit.'

I nodded.

'You're a nice guy and I'm a nice girl but that's about it. Nice and nice makes nothing.'

'You prepared that line.'

She laughed.

'Yes, I did. See that's the thing: I can admit that to you and you won't get mad. We're too polite to have fun.'

'Just me?'

'No, me too. I need someone down and dirty.'

'I could try,' I said but neither of us was convinced. So we kissed goodnight, said we'd see one another around and left it at that, knowing we wouldn't.

Thanksgiving came and Jake and his brother drove the five hundred miles to see their mother.

'Do it every year, expecting it to be the last but seems it never is,' Jake told me.

I was helping him clear out the year's accumulation of bags from the back of the barn. We took them out onto a headland and made a bonfire before he left.

'Some folks live beyond their time and some folks only get half a life. They're only getting out in the sun and then the sun goes down. Don't seem like there's any justice in that. Never seen the fairness in it. You take my mom. She's a bad-assed, nasty lady. Is why me and my brother is living five hundred miles from her. Be farther 'n that if we could find that place. And there she is, seventy-nine and still dipping life in a bucket o' shit for anyone she can.'

I'd never heard Jake talk so much at one time and as if he noticed my surprise, he added: 'Get like this every Thanksgiving – just the thought of seeing her. Me and my brother'll relax and smile when we pull out of her driveway and head for home. Always the best feeling of the whole damn holiday.'

I was sitting at the kitchen table that night, dawdling over dinner, and Emily said: 'You don't seem to go to town so much anymore.'

'No.'

'You were goin' in a lot, for a time.'

'Yes.'

'She dump you?'

'Hard to say,' I shrugged. 'Think we each dumped ourselves.'

'People expect too much from life. From love.'

'I don't think we came close to love,' I smiled.

'Sex then.'

I shook my head and laughed.

'You still want to sleep with me?' she asked.

'Yes,' I said but the word got lost in my throat.

She looked me straight in the eye, her dead blue stare holding me in its gaze.

'Yes,' I said again and this time the word came out too loud.

'I won't sleep with you,' she said quietly. 'But we can come to some arrangement, if you want, some kind of mutual satisfaction. You can watch and I can watch. That's all I can offer. No touching, no kissing, no lovemaking.'

'Why are you saying all this to me?'

'I've seen all the books you have down on the bunk house window,' she said. 'Reading books doesn't make you a better person. I used to read a lot of books and they had nothing to offer when it mattered. They were just mountains of letters, they meant nothing. And me saying this doesn't make me a bad person.'

'That's not what I meant.'

'What I'm offering you is the best I can offer. You don't know how far I've had to come to say what I've said.'

'I appreciate that.'

'Good of you.'

'We don't have to do anything,' I said, crossing my leg under me and leaning my chin on my hand.

She smiled that frozen smile.

'I'm not here to be analysed. Words mean whatever you want them to mean and that might, in the end, come down to absolutely nothing. If you want to do this, we'll do it. If you don't, that's okay. But it's not a negotiation. Some things are beyond all that and I'm not gonna to sit here and talk about it.'

'I'm sorry.'

'You say that a lot. It's another word.'

We held each other's gaze for a moment, two gunslingers on an empty street with nothing to lose and nothing, it seemed, to win.

'I'm going upstairs. If you want to follow, you're free to do that but I meant what I said.'

And that's how it began. It was easy for the four days Jake was gone, but afterwards, when it might have been more difficult, we found ways to make it possible. I'd go up to Emily's room, at the opposite end of the landing from her husband's room, and she'd lie on her bed and I'd sit in the big easy chair across from it and we'd masturbate. Sometimes it was mechanical, sometimes one or other of us got lost in the moment and occasionally we both forgot the distance between us, or were engrossed in the presence of the other, and were almost one or totally alone and it didn't seem to matter which. I never instigated anything; sometimes I wanted to but one look in Emily's eyes told me that I was the one who needed to wait; I would never be the one to drive this liaison.

Some days Emily was more reckless than others. She would bring me to her room while Jake was working in the barn and it was my responsibility to watch for his return. Sometimes this meant my rushing back downstairs and out the front door before he reached the yard door. And some days I'd see his tractor on the far horizon and know we were safe. Then I could look carefully at Emily, watch her fingers between her thighs, watch her breasts tighten and her nipples harden and listen to the chaos of her breathing as she came.

'*La petite mort*,' I said once as we were dressing. 'It's how the French describe this.'

'What does it mean?'

'The little death.'

She shuddered.

'I don't like that. Don't say that again. Please.'

I wondered, long after I'd left the farm, if our being caught together by Jake was inevitable – intentional even. Did I want him to find us? Did I fool myself into believing that discovery would force the moment and make Emily decide between her twilit world and the possibility of some other life, with or without me? Did she want her husband to know that not only had she rejected him but that she was being intimate with a stranger? Was what we were doing meant as a punishment that would, in time, find its target? Whatever our separate motives, he did find us.

An afternoon in early January, darkness falling, Emily and I lost in pleasure because, even then, those moments seemed of no consequence beyond their own fulfilment, minutes of isolated enjoyment taken out of ordinary lives, devoid of any connection to the past or the future, a time of engrossment.

What did Jake hear as he slowly climbed the stairs, his day's work done? At what point did he become aware of the urgent breathing from his wife's room? The bedroom door was open so he must have seen our figures from the turn of the stair, silhouetted against the picture window and the flat acres of land beyond. And as he reached the landing, he must have heard Emily moan and sigh, her body tightening like a fist and then exploding into relaxation as she came and he must have heard me say oh, fuck, fuck, fuck as I came.

I thought about all this afterwards but, in the moment of discovery, all I knew was that Emily's room was suddenly electric with light and she was lying naked on her bed, her hand still trapped between her legs and I was sitting naked in the easy chair by the window, my hand covering my limp, wet cock. And Jake was standing in the doorway, his face wearing an awful, wounded expression of disbelief and disappointment.

Emily looked her husband up and down and then rolled slowly on her side, her back to him. I froze. I waited for Jake to say something, to lunge across the room, but instead his gaze seemed to have strayed past his wife, past me and out onto the wintry landscape beyond the window.

I remember the awful uncertainty of that silence, and the feeling that he and Emily were less concerned by it than I was. And then Jake seemed to refocus, as though his mind were retracting like a telescope, changing his focal point and becoming aware, again, of what had been happening in his wife's bedroom.

He flicked off the light switch, turned and his heavy tread retreated along the landing. A door opened and a door closed and then there was an absolute stillness that seemed to mirror the stillness of the day outside. As the twilight settled in the room, the sky beyond became brighter. Through the window, nothing was moving. The trees were severe against the grey evening sky. I believed that if I reached out, I could touch the barn roof or open the bright red windows of the bunkhouse or run my hand along the chrome fender of my pick-up. Such was the stillness, such the clarity of that time.

Standing up, I began to twist into my jeans. Emily turned, flicked on her bedside lamp and picked through her clothes in that languorous way that women have, unhurried, considering each item as though it were brand new.

'Best you go,' she said quietly.

I nodded.

A door opened and there were footsteps along the landing. Pulling on my boots, I prepared myself for whatever was about to happen. Should I take my beating or put up a fight, try to run for it or talk my way out? Jake was standing in the doorway now. I stepped closer to the window, my shirt and jacket in my hand. And then I saw the bottle, a whiskey bottle, almost full, the neck tight in his fist. Emily went on dressing slowly, ignoring him. She stepped out of bed, pulled on her skirt and slipped her feet into her shoes. Jake watched her every move and only when she was dressed and ready to leave the room did he raise his arm and smash the bottle against the jamb of the door. The stench of whiskey flooded the room and Jake extended his arm, the jagged bottle top pointing first at me and then at Emily and then he smiled at her and said: 'Are we quits yet?'

She laughed – a low, dry laugh – and bent to lift her scarf from the floor.

Jake's arm angled slowly at the elbow and he buried the broken bottle in his throat, turning it this way and that, working the serrated glass into his flesh until the blood began to flow.

I shouted at him to stop and rushed across the room, grappling the bottle from his grasp, pulling it from his flesh as gently as I could and stuffing my shirt against the open wound.

'Call 911,' I said, but Emily didn't move. In that instant I realised she wasn't in shock; she simply had no interest in saving her husband's life.

Jake's body began to slide slowly down the jamb of the door. I moved with him, keeping the shirt tight against his neck, until he was sitting, his back against the wall, and I was kneeling beside him.

'Can you hear me, Jake?' I asked quietly.

He nodded.

'Can you hold the shirt if I call the medics?'

He nodded again.

'Keep it tight,' I said.

There were tears in his eyes and I wanted to hug him.

I ran down the stairs and dialled, gave the address and was back upstairs in under a minute. Jake was slumped against the wall but still conscious, the blood-soaked shirt pressed against his throat. Emily was sitting at her dressing table, slowly combing her hair.

I knelt beside him and whispered: 'You're going to be all right. Medics are on their way. Hang in there.'

His eyes were glazing over, breath stuttering through the wound in his throat.

'I'll turn the porch light on,' Emily said, stepping over him.

I stayed on at the farm for ten days more, until Jake was ready to come home. In that time I'd gone to see him twice at the hospital. I'd sat across the table from Emily and asked her why she had laughed at her husband when he'd found us together. I asked her a dozen times but she refused to speak to me.

In the middle of the second week, Jake's brother drove out from town to tell us Jake was being released the following day. Emily shrugged and carried on with what she was doing.

I walked Jake's brother back to his car.

'I don't know how much you know about what happened,' I said.

'Don't matter. That's not why he done what he done.'

'I wish I were that sure.'

'There's a history here,' he said, sitting on the hood of the car and opening a pack of cigarettes. He offered me one, took one himself and we lit up.

He drew deeply on his cigarette, scratched the back of his neck and surveyed the bunkhouse and the roof of the barn.

'No one to blame – just the way things catch up. Maybe now she'll be satisfied.'

He sucked again on his cigarette and it burned halfway down, the paper glowing and darkening.

'Was a little girl here one time, was killed in a wreck, Emily's daughter, not Jake's. He was driving. Too fast I reckon.' He pulled again on his cigarette, sucking it close to the filter before flicking it across the damp clay. 'She never got over it. Never forgave him. Guess the girl would've. She was a cute little thing. Smart as a lash.'

'So what's going to happen to them now?'

'Guess they'll pick up right where they left off. Wounding themselves and one another. What they been doing well for a long time now.'

'I'll move on.'

'Best for you. How's that pick-up of yours running?'

'Smooth.'

He smiled.

'I done a good job.'

'You did.'

'Best to leave all this kinda shit behind. Ain't no one ever gonna sort it.'

'I know.'

'You've been through it before?'

'Something like that.'

'Well you take it easy,' he said, pulling open his car door and sitting heavily in.

'You too.'

He turned the key, the engine hummed quietly, he waved, and then he was gone.

I packed my bags that night, threw them in the pick-up and walked up to the house.

Emily was sitting in the chair by the kitchen window.

'I'm going to move on,' I said. 'I think it's best for all of us.'

Her eyebrows arched.

'Jake's brother told me. About what happened.'

She nodded.

'Maybe now is a good time to forgive….'

'Don't,' she said sharply.

I stood in the middle of the kitchen and Emily sat where she was, looking out into the night.

'Right,' I said finally. 'Well then…I'll be going.'

I moved towards the door.

'Jessie,' she said, so quietly that I almost didn't hear.

'Nice name,' I said and then I opened the door and stepped out into the darkness.

The Word

A man stands by a narrow iron gate, his hand on the frost-locked bolt. Behind him, in the yard between his house and that gate, are the marks of his footsteps on the silent, fallen snow. Derelict sheds that once housed something and now house something else bound the yard on the other two sides. The man has not been inside these sheds in years. He hears wild animals scuttle through the rafters and across the rotting floors of the lofts but he wishes them well. He has his own space, a place in which to live, a house that is bigger than he ever needed, and he does not begrudge these other creatures their space.

It is a cold, bright, sunny morning in mid-March but as yet the spiked sunlight has not reached that area between the sheds. The grey shadow of stone and slate still sprawls across the cloistered ground. The man feels the murky coldness at his back, patting his overcoat with a dark, damp hand. He shivers, shakes the chilly branch off his shoulders, slides the bolt and steps into the churchyard. And the first things he notices are the daffodils, their tongues stretching for the golden sunlight that drips like paint all over them.

The man steps through the opening, leaving the gate unclosed behind him, and crosses the gravelled path to the door of a small and weathered church. A rope hangs straight and frozen against the wall and the man looks up, along its glistening line, as he does every Sunday morning, to the helmet of the bell, checking that it's still there. He smiles, as he often does, at this quaint, distrusting habit, grips the rope and begins the slow tolling that tells his listeners the service will begin in thirty minutes.

That done, he steps away, finds a key in his pocket and unlocks the double doors to the church. Inside, he walks quickly up the centre aisle, breathing deeply the dusty smell of antiquity and listening to the gulping belches of a central heating system that works against its own better judgement. In the vestry he lays out his surplice and soutane and marks the pages he will read from in the prayer book, before going back into the church to change the hymn numbers on their wooden shelves.

All this done, he walks back down the nave and out into the sunlight, aware that his parishioners will not begin arriving for at least twenty minutes. He smiles again, knowing the order in which they will come, the pews in which they will sit and the cacophony their voices will create once the organ grinds into life. But none of them is bitter and none of them is angry and he enjoys their idiosyncrasies, just as they put up with his. It has been this way for fifteen years and, he hopes, it will continue to be for at least another fifteen.

He wanders between the headstones in the burial ground, the 'shank-yard' as he heard one local describe it, reading the familiar names of unfamiliar parishioners who died a century or a decade or a month before his arrival. He knows their descendants, if there are any left, and he knows something of their history, sometimes from the stories he hears, sometimes from the registers of birth and marriage and baptism, and sometimes from the stones themselves.

He stops at one tombstone, which, in a decade and a half, has never ceased to chill him.

Sacred to the Memory
Of
Jennifer Stronge
Died Dec 17th 1918
Aged 8
Her sister Florence
Died Dec 20th 1918
Aged 13
Their brother Stephen
Died Dec 24th 1918
Aged 4
And their brother Marcus
Died December 28th 1918
Aged 11
Also their father Clarence
Died April 17th 1963
Aged 83.
They sleep in peace who sleep in the arms of the Lord.

At first, he had been perplexed. Now he knows the children died in the great flu, their father living on into seasoned old age. But what still intrigues him, a question that remains unanswered, is what happened to the children's mother. There are no records of her, other than her marriage certificate and references in the baptism certificates of her doomed children. Beyond that, nothing. And now there is no family to remember her, no parishioner who knows, or is willing to tell, the story of her last years. Did she flee in desperation? Were her last days spent behind the walls of some asylum? Was there some other story, of lust supplanting unspeakable grief? He has no idea but he prays each Sunday morning at this grave, recreating a brief life for the children where they play in the sun or the rain or the snow, their lungs clear, their eyes open, their laughter a welcome racket between the songbirds and the silence. He prays for the old man left alone for almost fifty years; he prays for the youngsters who tumbled down death's slide, one after the other, and he prays for the woman whose missing name is more eloquent than song.

And then he moves on, crossing the lawn where he knows he will someday be buried but he doesn't think about this. He has no anticipation of death – neither of the time of its arrival nor of its form. It will have to find him for he has no intention of searching it out, and that fact makes him smile from time to time.

He imagines the angel of death perched on one of the grander tombstones, scratching his head, having arrived to find the old priest on holiday and not having the faintest idea where to look for him. And in this fantasy, the angel squats for three days on the marble edifice before giving up and flying back whence he came. He likes the sound of that phrase – it says gravitas, it says frustration, it says he has eluded the dark feathered one again.

Reaching the hedgerow at the end of the graveyard, he scans the branches for early nests. In the months to come, he will return here day after day, to count the eggs, to see them hatch, to observe the chicks, to witness their first encumbered flights, to watch them flee the nest for the final time. By then the summer will have settled on the fields and these colder days will be long forgotten. He looks forward to the swagger of spring and the certainty of summer. He imagines himself here in his shirt sleeves, three months from now, cutting the grass between the tombstones, listening to the birds in the hedgerows, watching a blackbird intone from the highest branch of the tallest tree, and loving every moment of it.

He knows that fate might intervene and that he might not live to see that day, to watch that bird, to hear that song but he believes he will. There was a period in his life when he was perplexed by the question of how we know when the last times are. How do we recognise the last time we will see someone or the time we leave a place for good or know a smile is the last one we will ever see again?

Finally, in his fifties, he accepted that there is no way of knowing, no intuitive facility that allows the knowledge of last times and last things and his life has been much happier since then. He is calmer now and the darknesses have not come back.

He remembers those dark days, the hospitalisation, the friends coming to visit and, afterwards, when he began to rebuild the shaky edifice of his life, how they would call to his house with books. Each one had a book that would change his life for ever, the way it changed theirs. And then he took them with good grace and he read a few pages of each and he turned down the corners on pages he had never reached and he underlined trite phrases and truisms at random so that his friends, picking their gift from his bookshelves, would be happy believing that they had been right in their assessment of his mental state and, better still, that they had delivered the solution to his problems.

He moves on, travelling the length of the hedgerow, scanning the cold branches for further signs of life, for the outlines of newly built nests. Here and there, the buds are considering the possibility of pushing out into the early spring air but something delays them. Perhaps it's the snow on the ground or perhaps it's some other vestige of winter that lingers in the air, known only to the plants whose roots are buried in the cold earth.

Known too, perhaps, to the frozen corpses and the cold bones and the blind skulls which lie beneath the ground in this rich field, among them the dozens of people at whose funerals he officiated across the years. Is there some softening beneath the earth, metres down, that signals the start of spring and the conserved energy of growth as it begins the first huge push of another year, edging through the solid clay, urging whatever warmth it can muster from the earth's lost core, whispering in the dead ears of the long lost and the long forgotten while it passes on, climbing to the lighter sleepers who have been dead for only a decade or a year or a month, pressing the secret information into the roots of the whitethorn, the willow, the ash and the oak, encouraging the buds to shoot but not just yet?

He remembers his first funeral here and his uncertainty, searching for the right words to say, anxious at all costs to avoid the wrong words, the phrases that might be misinterpreted. And the later funerals where the formalities became less important and he could concern himself with the feelings of the bereaved and the achievements of the dead. He scans the ground before him and considers those he buried, those whose loss was little to him and those whose loss was great and he goes back beyond that, to the memory of a young woman with autumn leaves in her hair and a young man on a roadside, his blood pooled and puddled and how the dry earth of a faraway country sucked that blood as it might the juice of an overripe and fallen fruit.

He remembers the silences after both deaths.

The silence of the warm, winter hospital and the young woman's skin fading before his eyes, gold to sepia, then sepia to white and, finally, white to blue. And then the radiators in the overheated ward rumbling and groaning their beached whale-song for the dying and the dead. And her parents, unmoving and unspeaking, making a blessed trinity of frozen forms beneath the stinging light of the electric bulbs. He had stepped away from the bedside, pausing at the door to take in the last sight he would ever have of the young woman's face, and walked down the long pale corridor and out of their lives and their loss, crippled with the weight of his own.

And he remembers a day some months earlier when he had driven with the young woman into the Sangre de Cristo

Mountains. This woman whose name carried the history of Wales but whose home was Colorado. They had sat on the hood of her car, looking up at Blanca Peak, the cobalt snow like an invitation, the mountain range growing into its name as the sun began to slide down the back of the icy sky.

We were young and we were in love, he thought.

Thinking back on it now, it sounded like a line from a pop song but then it had said everything and, more importantly, it had meant everything.

He had told her about the Captain's death, about the way the blood had run along the warm sandy road and then down into the earth.

'Same way these mountains change colour?' she'd said.

He had thought about that for a while.

'More or less.'

'And?'

Again, he'd thought for a time.

'Some of the others believed that wasn't the end. They believed that something would survive; some of them even put a name on it.'

'What name?'

'The light. Startlingly original,' he had said sarcastically. 'I didn't believe that. I still don't. When he bled, that was it, as far as I'm concerned. Nothing more was left. It was over.'

'Perhaps it was a cultural thing– something your British reserve wouldn't allow,' she'd teased. 'Perhaps there's no room for certainty inside that head of yours. Bet you're wondering whether that colour on the range is really crimson or just an optical illusion. I'll bet you're not even certain the mountains are there.'

He'd smiled then, knowing she'd caught him, loving the way she could walk him out of his seriousness without his realising it was happening. And then she'd been serious again.

'So you really think, when the Captain died, that was the all of it?'

'Yes.'

'Nothing of his spirit survived after that afternoon on the road?'

'No.'

'We're talking about him now.'

'That's just my memory of things and your reaction to that memory; it's not something of him, just something about him. Words.'

'What about his words?'

'Words are words. Whether they're about someone or spoken by them, they're only words.'

'But they can affect people.'

'But that's the subjective response of the individual. You can't take words and say they'll have a universally common effect on people or any effect necessarily.'

'But what about those who did believe? What about the others who were with you – what about their belief?'

'Sometimes belief is just a fancy name for need.'

'Oh you cynic! What am I going to do with you?' she'd laughed, squeezing his arm and slapping it lightly.

And so they'd sat, holding hands, watching the mountains slice the sun until there was only a narrow arc left teetering on the horizon and she had shivered.

'You're cold,' he'd said. 'Let's go get some coffee.'

But neither of them had moved, each frozen in the moment, neither wanted to break the moment but each had other things on their mind, as he'd realised when it was all too late.

The mountain range became a dark stain on the sky and the colours of the evening trickled and streamed into each other before washing to a gentle, star-pricked blue.

He had sat, naively, stupidly, believing that they shared the same feelings. And, finally, when they got back into the young woman's car, he had smiled at her and kissed the side of her face and she asked: 'Are you happy?'

'Yes. Completely.'

'Really? I've never heard you use that word before.'

She'd laughed again.

'Completely,' he'd repeated.

They had driven to Las Animas County and she had taken him to a diner that she liked, a place where she felt comfortable, a place in which her parents would have been uneasy. But he'd been happy just to be there with her.

'Is this all too American for you?' she'd asked.

'Not everything American disturbs me.'

'Do I disturb you?'

'Only in the best possible way.'

And then she had told him, over the table of burritos and empanadas and guacamole. That she was dying. And he had listened and wished they were outside, that it was morning and that this day still lay ahead of them, that the rising sun was making sharp silhouettes on the sandy road outside his house. He had wished that at least the moon would rise through the night sky and throw some light on everything but there was no moon, only the vast and empty sky above the vast and empty Mojave desert.

She had seemed to read his mind.

'Don't you go thinking about that other desert and what happened to the Captain,' she'd said. 'This is different. That was a plane wreck. My death will be a slow and easy glide down to quietness. No blood. No corpse on the roadside.'

'How can you talk like that?' he'd asked. 'How can you talk like that about your own death?'

'Easy. It is my own death – that's the thing, that's why I can do it. I've thought about it, wrestled with it, been kicked by it, kicked back and now I'm cool with it. Worse things happen. Well they don't but the same thing happens in ways that are much worse.'

And then they'd driven back to his house and sat on the side of his bed and talked. And she had told him she wanted to enjoy the time that was left to enjoy; she didn't want him asking her about her illness, she didn't want him feeling sorry for her.

'Time enough for all that,' she'd said. 'Time enough when it gets to the stage where we can't do things. Let's be in the moment. I know your tight-ass Englishness doesn't easily allow you to do that and I know you hate the phrase but just do it, for me. Because you love me and I love you, that'll be the way we show it, okay?'

And he had nodded, although he didn't want to nod, although he had no idea what he wanted beyond being back at a time before he had known. But, when he thought about it, that had made him feel selfish because even back then she had known about it, she had been carrying the knowledge for days or weeks or months.

So he did what she asked and they enjoyed themselves. They drove up to Angel Fire and Eagle Nest and Red River, where they parked outside the Bull o' the Woods saloon and that afternoon they wandered down High Street and onto Independence Trail, crossing Main Street and down to Gilt Edge Trail and she had told him about growing up there and cycling her bike out Bitter Creek Road and round Stage Coach Bend. He had savoured these names, not because they were new to him but because they were familiar to her and he wanted to imbibe their familiarity, to carry the heat of the hot summer tar with him for ever.

The following night they'd camped at the Ghost Ranch and, lying in their tent, she had laughed.

'Here we are at Ghost Ranch. Waaaaahhhhhhh. Appropriate or what?'

'I wish you wouldn't be so flippant,' he'd said, regretting the words as soon as they were spoken.

'What choice do I have – moroseness? That's not a choice for me.'

'I know.'

'And I don't want it to be a choice for you.'

'What do you mean?'

'When this is all over, in a few months, when you go back to England, I don't want you to carry the weight of my memory on your shoulders.'

'You want me to forget you?'

'No. I want you to remember me in your heart. You told me, up at the mountain, that you were completely happy.'

'I was.'

'I want you to carry me as that happiness inside you. Not the crap stuff, just that. Can you do that for me? That you keep me inside you as happiness, contentment?'

He hadn't answered but she asked him again, seven weeks later, in her hospital room and he had said yes not to placate her but because he wanted her to be with him in that way for the rest of his life.

'If you can believe that I'm there with you, you can believe anything,' she'd whispered and they had smiled and she had kissed him with her last, living kiss.

And afterwards it had taken him years to find the strength to trust his life to her but, in the end, he had done it.

The man crosses the cold, frosted grass and steps, again, inside the church, his church.

The radiators are still muttering and grumbling but he ignores them and goes to the book on the lectern and turns to Matthew 6:34.

Take therefore no thought for the morrow: for the morrow shall take thought for the things of itself. Sufficient unto the day is the evil thereof.

He imagines her laughing, telling him that's what she said and asking why he needs to find validation in a book and, in that instant, he sees her face again, as clear and as pale and more beautiful even in illness than it was in health. He smiles a small, warm smile and remembers one of the last conversations he had with the young woman. She was lying in the high white hospital bed and he was sitting in the low armchair, a blanket pulled about him against the air-conditioned, night-time chill. He dozes off and when he wakes he sees her bright green eyes staring into his and he winks and she winks back.

'You think this a waste, don't you?' she asks.

'What's a waste?'

'My life ending like this.'

'I'll miss you.'

She smiles that warm, fragile smile.

'I won't be gone for ever. There'll be a time.'

'Will there?'

'Yes.'

'I wish I could believe that,' he says and immediately regrets his words. 'But you believe there will be and that's good, that's positive, that's a good belief to have.'

'You're bullshitting,' she laughs.

'I am.'

He leans forward and takes her hand in his. He can smell the sickness from her breath as he kisses her, his tongue tracing the shape of her tongue. His fingers glide across her head, taking clusters of red hair with them.

'You know,' she says quietly. 'No life is incomplete. I don't feel I haven't reached the end. I feel I'm getting close to the place that is the end for me, that's all. There's more than one place to finish.'

'I like that idea,' he says.

She is silent for a while, still watching him, her glowing eyes following his. At last she speaks: 'Are you all right?'

'I'm okay.'

'I've asked you before but I'll ask again, are you happy?'
He shrugs.
'I tend to draw my happiness from others.'
'And your sadness?'
'From myself.'
'That's not good.'
'No.'
'But....'
'But if you were well, I'd be really happy, all the time.'
Again, the silence between them and her eyes on his and his eyes filling with tears.
'Will you promise me something?' she asks.
'If I can.'
'That you'll try to believe that we'll meet again, that you'll draw on that hope, that it'll keep you happy for most of the rest of your life.'
'I will try. I'll really, really try. You have my word.'

And he had tried and out of somewhere the acceptance started to come, not always but often enough to give him a direction in his life. And gradually that belief became a kind of happiness and he lived his life in expectation of a happy ending.

Now and then sadness got in the way of the hope but, mostly, he was all right.

Once, in his second or third year in this parish, he had officiated at the funeral of a local woman. He had known her but not particularly well and had conducted the service with the warmth and recognition that her life deserved. He had spoken about her love of nature, her eye for detail, her gift for painting and her openness to the world. And then her son had said a few words, talking of her birthplace in Wales and of how, though she had been away from it for forty-seven years, she had always hankered to go back. And then the young man began to sing his mother's favourite song and the priest had sat and listened, feeling the tears well in his eyes, sensing all the years of hope and trust wash away as the tune rose and swelled and the Welsh words swept like a flood across the sanctuary.

> *Myfanwy, may you spend your lifetime*
> *beneath the midday sunshine's glow,*
> *and, on your cheeks, O may the roses*
> *dance for a hundred years or so.*
> *Forget now all the words of promise*
> *you made to one who loved you well,*
> *give me your hand, my sweet Myfanwy,*
> *but one last time, to say 'farewell'.*

When the song ended, he sat for a long time, composing himself, reminding himself that the family members of this dead woman were the ones in need of consolation and then he rose, walked to the lectern and thanked the young man for his words and for the beauty of the song.

'We draw hope from those who have gone before us,' he said quietly. 'Just that, but often that is enough.'

He hears the church door open and voices from the porch and he steps into the vestry, leaving the early comers to their own conversations. Pulling open the small window in the vestry wall, he breathes in the deep morning coldness from outside and steadies himself against the ancient, rickety table with its nest of collecting plates.

In the pulpit, he stands, counting the greying heads below him, two dozen souls in search of something.

'It would be easy for me to stand here and preach to you about how you should live your lives but I won't,' he began. 'They say that at three o'clock in the morning we are at the lowest point in our resistance – sometimes three o'clock is the depth of darkness. But sometimes three o'clock shows a lightness in the summer sky that says day. There is always the struggle but the struggle is often worthwhile. I once read something that Emerson wrote: Our faith comes in moments, our vice is habitual. At the time it rang a bell with me. But I look back now and I realise that I have been blessed, in the last fifteen years, with a life of happiness and that, too, has become habitual. I didn't expect it to be so but I'm happy that it has been. I wish each and every one of you the same.'

And then he pauses, smiles and steps from the pulpit.

The organist begins playing a hymn, very badly, out of time and out of tune.

I'm sure God, if there is a God, hates the sound of the organ, he thinks.

'Well you caught me on the hop, Padre,' one of the older men in the congregation huffs as they shake hands at the church door. 'Just settling myself for a nap and bang the whole thing was over, short and sharp like a … like a … like whatever it is that's short and sharp. Well, let's not go there, as they say. Good job.'

'Thank you,' he says.

'Keep it up. No point in gilding the lily. I hope this is the start of a trend.'

'Ah, but then you'd be pining for the extended version, Frank.'

'Don't think so. Let's continue as is. At ease.'

He locks the church door and crosses the gravel path, darker now as it becomes a melting shadow in the late morning sun. He quietly closes the gate behind him and retraces his steps through the light snow, banging the toes of his boots on the step outside his hall door before going inside.

In the kitchen, he fills the kettle and turns on the gas, one ring beneath the kettle, one ring beneath the saucepan of potatoes. He checks on his small Sunday roast in the oven. All is well. The kettles sings and spits and he makes himself a cup of tea and takes it into the drawing room. He sits in his favourite chair, looking out through the double glass door onto the frozen, white lawn and the sallow birch trees beyond. He watches the birds hanging upside down from the feeders and ticks their names on the list that sits on the arm of his chair. Robin, thrush, redwing, sparrow, blackbird, crow, blue-tit, great-tit.

'All present and correct,' he mimics Frank quietly.

He scribbles quickly: If there is a God, we do him a disservice by not questioning him. If there isn't a God, we do ourselves a disservice by not questioning him.

The sparrows squabble and throw their tiny weights about, unafraid of anything. He envies them. A crow stands to one side, head cocked, glowering. He understands the bird. The redwing goes about the business of eating. The blackbird stabs an apple. Each is driven by its own eccentricity.

He notices that the calendar on the sideboard is a month out of date and gets out of his chair, crossing to flick the page and read the aphorism for February. If winter comes, can spring be far behind?

'Deep and meaningless,' he says out loud.

And then he lifts a framed photograph from the sideboard and stares at the figure of a man dressed in the loose trousers and light shirt of a summer in the thirties. The man sits in a meadow scattered with sepia flowers. Seated beside him are two sheepdogs; another stands behind him, staring suspiciously over his shoulder at the photographer. This is his Uncle Thomas, the man after whom he was named, a man he never met but with whom he feels a great affinity, not of name but in the dogs by his side, never at his feet, there as equals. There are seven photos of Uncle Thomas in this house and in each one there are dogs, always at ease in his company.

Returning to his chair, he sits watching the birds plunge and plummet and he remembers a day in boarding school, an afternoon in November, sitting in a classroom, listening while his favourite teacher read from the class anthology and dictated notes on the poem, lost in the awful sadness of Byron's words.

So we'll go no more a-roving
So late into the night,
Though the heart be still as loving
And the moon be still as bright.
For the sword outwears its sheath
And the soul outwears its breast,
And the heart must pause to breathe
And love itself have rest.

'Are you taking notes?' the teacher had asked, his tone unchanging.

'No, sir. There are notes at the back of the book,' he had answered naively.

'Up here,' the teacher signalled and he had stepped out of his desk and gone to stand at the front of the classroom. But, as he reached the teacher, the man's fist shot out and sent him reeling across the front row of desks. One of the boys screamed and ran from the room. Thomas began to struggle to his feet, head spinning, feet unsteady. Another of his classmates stepped into the aisle and steadied him.

'Back to your desk,' the teacher said, his voice terrifyingly placid. 'And take notes.'

He had walked slowly, not wanting to fall, not certain he could maintain his balance, and sat heavily into his seat, the side of his face reddening and stinging where the teacher's fist had caught him.

Then the soothing voice again:

Though the night was made for loving
and the day returns too soon,
yet we'll go no more a-roving
by the light of the moon.

'Fucking words!' he says out loud.

But words have been his only defence against the darkness he has held at bay for every minute of every day since she died and now their sheen is gone, their worth has been tested beyond endurance. They have become a shabby shroud of armour, no longer capable of sustaining him against the hopelessness that has trailed him all these years. And, as the tears begin to fall, the birds outside his window become a blur, their colours running into one another, their flight a lost, uncertain smear. The day has come again, the Captain's blood runs, wasted on the yellow sand.

My Beloved Son

I remember the evening well; it was in the winter of the sixth year after the Captain had been killed. We were in the library together, my young son James and me. Same name, same blood. And the librarian, a really nice woman, always smiling, always saying hello when we came in to play chess, was gathering up the books and I had one eye on the clock, knowing the place would close in fifteen minutes.

'It's lovely to see you here with your boy,' she said quietly.

She looked at James.

'You and your dad are really close,' she said.

He smiled and nodded and then his attention went back to the board.

'Anyway, I just wanted to say that,' the librarian added. 'I've been meaning to say it for weeks.'

I noticed that she had a really warm smile and her dark hair fell around her face as she stooped to pick some books from the table beside ours.

'You keep playing,' she said. 'I won't be finished tidying till ten past, so take your time and enjoy your game.'

'Thank you,' I said.

Did she know, I wondered? How could she – it's a big town with a lot of people coming and going. She couldn't know.

'Check,' James whispered.

I studied the board but there was nothing I could do; no move I could make that would get me out of the noose he had made for me.

'Looks like you might have me caught.'

He smiled and sat back, folding his arms, and it was worth being checkmated to see that satisfaction, that smile.

'I'll just make sure,' I said, though I knew it was a hopeless task and James knew that I knew. He clasped his hands behind his back, looked nonchalantly around him and went on grinning. I examined the board, piece by piece, possibility by possibility, but there was nothing to be done.

'You got me,' I said.

'Again.'

'Again. What's that, four in a row?'

'Five.'

'Is it?'

'You know it is.'

We began to put the pieces back in the box, carefully laying each one in its compartment, James the white pieces, me the black.

'All done?' the librarian asked, coming back to our table.

'All done,' I said.

'Who won?'

'Need you ask?'

'Five in a row, between last Thursday and tonight,' James said.

'You're obviously a very good player.'

James blushed.

'And thank you for putting the pieces away,' she added.

'We always do,' James said.

'I know. I've noticed. Not everyone does.'

'And thank you,' I said. 'You make us welcome.'

'We'll see you on Thursday,' she said.

I nodded and pulled on my jacket and hat.

'Cold outside,' she said. 'Freezing again.'

'Yes.'

'Well, take care. See you on Thursday.'

'Thank you.'

'Thank you,' James said.

'Some night you'd better let your daddy win,' the librarian winked as we headed for the door.

'Should I let you win, Dad?'

We were walking the bitter street, the wind tunnelling into our faces, an ambulance screaming in the distance.

'No, you should not. The lady was just being kind to me. You're a good player, James. You keep working on your game. You deserve to win. You think things through.'

'I'm glad you came back,' he said.

I took his small, gloved hand in mine and squeezed it.

'Me too.'

'Was it warm in that country?'

'Very.'

'Did you like that?'

'I liked the heat but I missed you.'

'Do you miss the Captain?'

'Yes,' I said. 'I do miss him but not in the same way I missed you.'

'And I wasn't dead. I was only in a different country.'

'You're right.'

I rubbed his head, tousling the hair beneath his woolly hat, pushing it down into his eyes while he laughed uproariously, his sweet ten-year-old voice ringing in the empty street.

We walked on, hand in hand, James peppering me with questions about the Captain, as he often did. What was he like? Were you there when he was killed? Was he ever funny? Was his mother very sad when he was killed? Was he very brave? Are you braver than he was? Did you nearly get killed too? Were you afraid?

I answered truthfully the questions I could. The rest I glossed over.

And then we were at the gate of his mother's house and we were hugging and he held me tightly, his little arms trying to encircle me, his hands making fists of the back of my jacket.

'I'll be here on Thursday night. At the gate. Six o'clock. You can count on it.'

'Sharpish.'

'Sharp.'

'Sharpest.'

'On the nail.'

'On the button.'

We had this rigmarole we went through every time I left him home.

'Can I come and stay with you some night?'

He hadn't asked me that in over a month.

'Soon now, yes, soon.'

'That'll be nice. We can watch TV.'

'Yes.'

'Goodnight, Daddy.'

'Goodnight, my son.'

We hugged again and he galloped up the path and I waited till the hall door had opened and closed before I turned away from the gate and retraced my steps along the avenue, leaving the multi-coloured houses behind, crossing the bridge and out onto the street that would take me to the other side of town.

I was living in a shed back then. But, as far as I was aware, only three people knew: James's mother, the elderly man who owned the shed and myself. The man had made it as habitable as he could. He'd put a stove in the corner and a bed beside that and a padlock on the door. It was the best he could do and I was happy to have it. He didn't charge me any rent and the place was secure, all the more so because no one else knew I lived there. I showered at the swimming pool and spent my days on the move, looking for work, taking whatever odd jobs came my way, sometimes finding two or three weeks on a farm or as a builder's labourer in other towns, not letting things get to me, always coming back on the nights I was due to collect James. But it wasn't the kind of place his mother would ever allow our son to stay and she made that perfectly clear, as though I'd ever think of bringing him there and didn't have any pride left.

So, on Tuesdays and Thursdays we went to the library and played chess. Saturday afternoons we went to a film or, if the weather was good, we cycled or walked out into the country. And once a week I'd go to the bank and lodge what I'd saved that week into my account.

Sometimes I offered rent to the man who owned the shed but he'd just smile and tell me not to be crazy, that I was keeping it aired against the future. So once a month I'd drop something to his house – a bottle of whiskey or a box of strawberries or a cowboy book. He liked westerns. And he'd say: 'There's no need.' And I'd say: 'Least I can do.' And he'd say: 'You're keeping that place aired against the future.' And sometimes I'd come home and find a piece of furniture outside the door, an armchair or a table or a locker. He'd never unlock the door, never intrude into what he saw as my place, just leave it outside, wrapped in plastic if the day was wet.

So, week by week and month by month, I put money aside and by the end of the year I had enough saved to lease a flat but I didn't. I went on saving and I started telling James about the house I was going to rent. It would have a bedroom for me and one for him when he came to stay, but I never told him about the shed.

'And can you have a TV in your bedroom?' he asked excitedly. 'And can we watch it in bed at night? Late. Sometimes Mammy lets me do that, sometimes we watch TV together. At weekends.'

'Course we can.'

'When will you get your new house?'

'At the end of winter.'

'And will we stop going to the library?'

'What do you think?'

He shook his head.

'I like it there. I like the lady.'

'I agree but when the library closes, we can go back to my house for hot chocolate and you can stay there at weekends, if your mum says it's okay.'

And that's how it was. I found a place to rent and when I approached the owner of the shed about doing a deal to buy the bits and pieces of furniture he'd provided, he wouldn't hear of taking any money.

'Not a question about it. They're yours.'

And on the day I was moving, he brought his van down to the shed and loaded the furniture with me. On the last run, after he'd gone home, supposedly to have his lunch, he returned with a three-piece suite in the van.

'It was doing nothing where it was,' he said. 'You'll get some use out of it. The young fellow can sleep on the couch when he comes to see you.'

'Thank you.'

'No need, no need.' He waved away my thanks, not dismissively but because he was embarrassed. '"From each according to his ability…"'

'"…to each according to his need,"' I finished.

'I knew you were a good man,' he said and then we got on with unloading the furniture.

When the work was done, we sat on the back step, looking onto the small garden. I pointed out what I was going to plant and where.

He got up and walked across the garden, digging it with his boot heel, rubbing the soil between his fingers.

'Needs manure,' he said. 'Dead as a doornail. I'll drop some up.'

'You have enough to do.'

'Well it won't grow anything otherwise. Dig it in, dig it well in. Let it break down, it'll make a big difference.'

The following evening, when I got home from work, there were eight plastic sacks of manure stacked against the side wall of the house and a fork laid across them.

I smiled at that. Typical, I thought. He won't brook any excuses.

I hadn't dug in years but I enjoyed the work and during my working day, while I was barrowing blocks for the block layers, I looked forward to the evening and the work I'd be doing in my garden. I couldn't wait to go out and get the sods turned; the grass piled and dried in a corner, ready for burning; the soil turned and the manure dug in. One evening, a young couple with a baby next door came and stood at the fence and chatted while I rested between digging and spreading.

'I must do something with this place,' the young man said, eyeing the wilderness on their side of the fence.

'You renting or do you own?' I asked.

'Renting,' the young woman said quickly.

'Same as myself.'

'Ah, right.'

'I'll give you a hand, if you like,' I said. 'Once I get this place done.'

'Not at all,' the young man said. 'I'll get stuck into it next week. You have enough to be doing there.'

'Well, once it's sown, there won't be much else I can do, apart from keeping it weeded. So just say the word.'

'Well, I might do that. Thanks.'

The young woman looked at him and then looked away.

By the time James came to stay for his first overnight, the garden was a glorious flicker of browns, reds, blues and greens, the sun picking shades and shadows in the late spring evening. And a week later the drills and beds were made and a week after that we worked together, kneeling in the warm soil to sow seeds and then raking beds and dreaming of the crops that lay, still curled inside their seed pods, beneath the ground.

I never did get to help the couple next door. I saw them one morning, early the following week, loaded down with suitcases and plastic sacks, pushing the baby's buggy out the front gate. It was six o'clock and they were heading for the early train.

I pulled on my jacket, went out and took three or four of the bags and walked with them to the station. They didn't speak and neither did I but I knew, by the way they were laden down, that this was a flitting. At the station, just as the train pulled in, I stuck a fifty note in the young woman's hand and legged it. The last thing I saw was the couple loading their bits and bags onto the train and the young man lifting the buggy through the open doorway.

Another evening, early that summer, when the plants began to grow, I invited the Shed-man, as I thought of him, to come to dinner. He inspected the drills and beds and told me I'd done myself proud and that the garden was a credit to me.

'Your dad is a hard worker,' he told James. 'You're a lucky young man to have him for a father and to share his name with him too. Doubly blessed. And he's lucky to have you.'

Later when I talked about the Shed-man, James asked me why I called him that.

'I stored some furniture in his shed once,' I lied. 'He's a nice man.'

'Why don't you ask him his name?'

'His name is George.'

'So why don't you say George?'

'You're right, I should. I will.'

And I did. The next time he visited, I called James from the garden.

'George is here. He has something for you.'

The old man had brought a bag of sweets for James and a box of strawberry plants for me for the garden. While we planted them, he nodded towards the house next door.

'I hear they did a runner?'

'They did,' I said. 'To tell you the truth, I felt sorry for them. I carried some of their bags to the station. I guessed they were getting away.'

'Good man.'

He settled a plant in the soil and firmed the earth about it, took another from the box and did the same.

'Never liked the fellow who owns that place,' he said, sitting back on his heels.

'You know him?'

'I do. I saw him shoot one of his dogs one time because he thought it was ugly. A man that'd do that deserves no sympathy. A man that'd do that would do anything.'

That spring, two magpies lived their joyous life on a quiet country road and every morning I'd see them, black and white, while I cycled to work. By the time June came, my garden was productive enough to promise food for the rest of the summer. I had built a small greenhouse from bits and pieces of timber and a few old window frames that I'd taken from an out-office we were demolishing on the building site. Green tomatoes bunched against the glass, lettuces and scallions were a month ahead of the lettuces and scallions in the open drills. Potatoes and peas and runner beans flowered at the far end of the garden, away from the house. Closer to the back door, I had sown onions, parsnips, turnips, beetroots and carrots in a sandy bed.

'You'll never eat them all,' George had laughed and I knew he might be right but I'd found it hard to pass a seed packet without wanting to try another variety.

'And you won't go hungry,' I promised.

Along the fence, between the still vacant neighbouring house and my own, I'd sown sunflowers. They, too, were pushing up and each weekend James had the job of measuring them. There were ten in all and we'd given them the names of other flowers.

'Pansy is leading,' he'd tell me. 'But she gets more sun and later in the day.'

'So that's why!'

He nodded.

'And why is Lily coming last? She's in the middle, not brightest, not darkest.'

He thought about that for a moment.

'Soil,' he said. 'Bet there's a concrete block under her.'

I laughed. He sounded just like George.

'Am I probably right?'

'You're probably right,' I said.

One evening, in the middle of July, as I was about to take my bike out and cycle up to collect James, the phone rang. It was his mother. I hadn't spoken to her, nor had I heard her voice, in more than five years. We had communicated through her solicitor, arranging access and collection times and dates. But the moment she said my name, I knew who she was.

'You're due to collect James,' she said.

'Yes. Is everything all right?'

'Everything is fine. I just thought I could save you the journey. I could drive him over. If that's acceptable.'

'Of course. That would be fine.'

'We'll be there in ten minutes.'

I left the front door open and each time a car slowed, I stepped out onto the front garden path. Eventually, her car drew up at the gate and I saw James in the passenger seat. To my surprise, his mother got out and walked up the path with him, smiling.

'I've heard great things about your garden. James tells me you've been working hard.'

'Can Mum see it?' James asked.

'Of course she can.'

I'd been lost in the fact that for the first time in five years I was having a civil conversation with this woman who had once been my wife and lover and had, with good reason, come to hate me.

I led them through the house and into the back garden and, as we stepped into the sunlight, I felt proud of the work I'd done over the previous months. Everything was growing, everything looked healthy.

'And we have sunflowers,' James said.

'So I see,' his mother said and then she turned to me. 'You've done a wonderful job. You should be proud of it.'

'I suppose I am,' I said and I tried to smile but no smile came, only a sense of abject self-loathing.

'Will I put the kettle on, Dad?'

'Do,' I said. 'I'm sure everyone would like a cup of tea.'

He scampered inside and his mother walked between the drills and beds.

'You've packed an amazing amount into a small space.'

'Thank you. There's more than I'll need. You're welcome to anything you want.'

'And James says you're well.'

'I'm well, thank you.'

'Good,' and then an abrupt silence that sprawled awkwardly.

We stood in the evening sun, the full light of July breaking over us in one long, warm wave. She leaned across suddenly and lifted my T-shirt, looking at the twisted scar that seemed still raw after all these years, the place where a blade of bullets had ripped my flesh and left me bleeding on the roadside, my blood running with the Captain's into the ground.

'How's the pain?' she asked tentatively, as though she were afraid the answer might be the one she had heard in the years before we parted.

'The pain is manageable. It's never going away but I cope with it, on my own, without anything. I'm not just saying that.... I appreciate your coming around with James.'

As though on cue, our son appeared at the back door and called us. We went inside together and sat in the kitchen, drinking tea, eating biscuits, perhaps even happy in the moment. And afterwards I walked James's mother down the path and thanked her again for visiting.

'You don't have to call but I'd be happy if you did,' I said, as she sat into the car.

'We'll see,' she said. 'And it's good to see you so well. I'm glad you're well.'

I nodded. She pulled on her seat belt.

'And I'm glad you let me find James again and get to know him.'

'You're a good man,' she said. 'You just did things I couldn't handle. I know it was the pain and the medication and all that stuff but it wasn't up to me to deal with it. You were dangerous, you were vicious and not just that night. I'm not saying that to make you feel guilty. I just need to say it.'

'I was. I hope I never am again.'

'I hope so too.'

Later, after we'd watered the plants and measured the sunflowers and I'd dropped James to his gate, I sat in the open back doorway of my house, cradling a mug of tea, and I thought about the last time, before this evening, that I'd talked to James's mother.

It was a wet night and we were sitting in my car in the car park of a rundown hotel and, in the end, not because of the pain or the medication or the loss of love, not because I had run out of words but simply because I could think of nothing else to do, nothing that would make her see how badly I needed her not to go, because the anger overcame the pain, I hit her. My fist caught the side of her face. Not my hand or my fingers but a closed fist that bounced back off her cheekbone. It took her a couple of seconds to recover from the blow and by then blood was trickling from a cut beneath her eye and I was thinking of the Captain's blood and my blood on the sandy yellow road.

'Now you know,' I said. 'Now you have some fucking notion of what it feels like.'

And then she opened the door of my car and stepped out into the rain. I didn't try to stop her, didn't say anything, didn't laugh or cry or shout. I just sat there and watched her walking. The dribbling rain on the windscreen began to melt her form but still I did nothing. When she reached her car, I saw her fumble in her bag for her keys and then I saw her wipe her cheek with the sleeve of her jumper before the hazard lights flashed and she sat in.

It took her twenty or thirty seconds to start the engine but I knew she wasn't waiting for my apology, wasn't hoping I'd cross the car park and try to explain away this new cruelty. I knew she was catching her breath, feeling the tender skin and the bruised bone beneath the blood. She was trying to gather the strength and the courage and the calmness to drive away. And then she did, as she had done on a hundred other nights when we said goodbye – sometimes kissing; sometimes touching; sometimes embracing in the cold or warm night air; sometimes, lately, fighting about the painkillers I couldn't live without. And the car drifted out, an unsteady haze at the hotel gate, and then it disappeared. I leaned across and pulled the passenger door closed and took a packet of tablets from my pocket and a bottle of brandy from under my seat and I swallowed the tablets and drank the brandy until there was only a cupful in the base of the bottle.

Stepping out of the car, I splashed what remained of the brandy on the driver's seat, struck a match and waited for the flames to catch. Only then did I close the door and walk away, not looking back, not buttoning my coat against the rain, not doing anything. An hour later, I lay down in the deep porch of a church and the Captain's words came back to me. A man's enemies will be in his own house.

I had no memory of when he'd said it but I knew the words were his and I knew, with the terrible clarity that sometimes came out of the haze of pain and numbness, that this was what he had meant, that this woman would never understand what we had been through, not just the Captain's death and my festered wound but the years of camaraderie, the months when our belief was not just a dream or an aspiration but something achievable, something of significance and consequence.

And then I fell into a deep, satisfied sleep and I dreamed, and in my dream there was no rain, no woman walking away, no tomorrow when she would have to invent a story about her wounded face for our son, no years when I drifted out of his life and he grew from childhood to being a small boy, nothing of the years of violence and jail and anger and dependence, nothing of the realisation that the next step would be my last – none of that. And nothing of my slow rehabilitation and the years living in that shed which became a place of unexpected redemption, nothing of the tentative approaches to see our son again, a handsome boy of eight with the weight of my absence laid heavily on his heart – none of that.

And, for that minute, sadness drained me, sucking every morsel of hope and happiness from my heart. Then, looking over my shoulder, I saw the three cups and saucers, the biscuit plate, the milk carton and the sugar bowl, domestic promises on a kitchen table, and I allowed anticipation and desire to lodge again within me.

In late July, George and James and myself dug the first potatoes, cooked them and sat in the kitchen eating them, smothered in butter and sprinkled with salt. James watched as George and I ate them, skins and all.

'Can you eat the jackets?'

'Best part,' George smiled. 'Try one.'

I laughed while James tentatively tasted a piece of skin and then another, chewing uncertainly but surprised, it seemed, by how tasty it was.

That night, when I dropped him home, he took a bag of potatoes with him for his mother.

'Will Mum know you can eat the jackets?'

'I think she will.'

'They taste okay.'

'They do.'

'And we sowed them, Dad, didn't we?'

'We did. You and me.'

He smiled and gripped my hand a little tighter.

In early August, James's mother came to see the sunflowers open and follow the sun. She spent an afternoon with us and we ate in the garden, James and myself carrying the table onto the small patch of grass and serving a meal that consisted only of produce we'd grown ourselves. George joined us and charmed James's mother with his courtesy and gentle humour.

'That man is good for you,' she said as she was leaving.

'And good for James.'

She nodded.

James walked ahead of us, carrying two baskets of vegetables to the car.

'Thank you,' she said and she kissed me lightly on the cheek.

Despite the warmth of the setting sun, I felt myself go cold and she noticed the shiver flooding through me.

'I'm sorry,' she said. 'I shouldn't have done that. Are you okay?'

'Yes,' I nodded. 'But sorry…so sorry.'

And that was all I could say because it was the truth.

In September I brought James with me when I collected a second-hand car from the garage on the edge of town. The number plate said it was seven years old but the smell inside was the smell of a new car. We drove to his mother's house and she came out and said all the things we wanted to hear and told us we looked the right pair in it.

'Like pilots ready for take-off.'

'Isn't it cool, Mum?' James asked.

'Super cool,' she said. 'It was made for the two of you. And it seems like it's been well looked after. Well wear.'

'Thank you,' I said and I knew, in that instant, that we were both thinking of the night I'd burned my last car and I was hoping she could believe that I was truly different now, that although the pain in my body and the pain in my soul would never go away, I could live with them and not be at their beck and call.

'You should come in for a cup of coffee,' she said when she'd walked around the car a few more times.

'Is that a good idea?'

'I think it's something we can do.'

And we did, we sat again, the three of us, and she and I listened while James talked about the places we could drive to.

'The zoo, the sea, the mountains, somewhere no one has ever been, the place where the country ends, loads of places and we could all go and one time we could take Mum's car and the next time yours and then when I'm big enough to have my own car, I can bring the two of you in my car.'

I said nothing.

'Sounds good,' his mother said. 'We'll talk about it.'

Maybe we only know heaven when we've left it. Maybe that's all it is, a point of reference that crops up in our lives. Perhaps that's why it's not a lasting kingdom. All it ever can be is a place we look fondly back on or a place to which we aspire but not a place we're ever permitted to stay.

It was the first Friday in September and I'd collected James from his mother's house. We were driving back to my house to do a final measurement on the sunflowers. George would meet us there to act as arbiter, in case of any disagreements.

'Who do you think will win?'

'Iris or Pansy or Lily. They've all made a late burst.'

'But Pansy has the biggest face!'

'She has, no doubt about that.'

'It's exciting.'

'It is.'

We stuttered through the evening traffic.

'Would you like some fish and chips?' I asked.

James's face and eyes lit up and his fingers spread wide, his teeth gritted in a mock grimace. I fumbled in my pocket and found a note.

'You hop out here and order three cod and chips and I'll find a parking space and meet you at the chipper.'

He opened the door.

'Does George take salt and vinegar?'

'He does.'

'Okay.'

I watched him cross carefully to the opposite path and disappear inside the shop. The traffic budged and stuck and budged and stuck until, at last, I could turn onto a one-way street and find a parking space behind the library. I locked the car and ambled back the way I'd come, past the railings outside the bank that made a zebra of the sunny evening road. Past the empty, broken window of a derelict shop and out onto Main Street. And then I heard the screaming. At first I thought it was the high pitch of a girl's laugh, but it went on, unrelenting. A scream that was pitted only by someone catching their breath before it gathered force again, rising and faltering between desolation and horror. The traffic had come to a halt and some people were standing by the open doors of their cars, staring down the length of the street, as though they were waiting for some great question to be resolved. And the screaming went on and on and I followed its reverberation across the street and into the open doorway of the chip shop.

The screaming woman was standing at the deep fat fryer, her face the white of lard. A second woman was on the phone at the back of the shop. There was no one else behind the counter. The owner and two other women who worked in the shop were on their knees outside the counter, bloodied tea towels in their hands. One of them was bent low, pushing air into someone's lungs. And then I saw James's jeans stretched between the shapes of these three people, his blue runners angled clumsily, one of his legs shuddering spastically. Abruptly, the screaming woman stopped screaming, as though she had lost all the energy she needed to carry on, and there was silence, apart from the sound of the kneeling woman breathing into my son's mouth and the dull hum of cars in the street.

'Did you call the ambulance?' the owner shouted.

'Yes,' the woman who'd been on the phone said. 'It's on its way.'

'That's my son,' I said.

The man looked up at me, terrified.

'The guy came to get money. I gave him the money,' he said. 'I gave it all to him.'

I could see the hole in James's shirt and the dark blood on the black and white tiles of the floor, and the red blood on his skin, and the awful colour of his face, a colour I'd seen only once before.

'The guy was turning to leave,' the man said. 'He was turning to walk away. I don't know why he fired, I don't know why. He blew the little boy off his feet. I gave him all the money. Gave him everything. I didn't even argue, they'll tell you.'

'That's my son,' I said again, as though neither of us was hearing the other. 'That's my little boy.'

After the funeral, we went back to my house, the three of us. For no better reason than that I was driving. And we sat in silence in the kitchen and then George got up and made three mugs of coffee and they went cold on the table between us.

I don't know what the other two were thinking but I was trying to figure out why a man with money in one hand and a gun in the other would shoot a small boy dead, and I couldn't find even the beginning of an answer.

After the little box had been buried, with our son inside it, the shop owner had come up to us at the graveside. For a long time he said nothing and when he spoke the only words that came out were the ones he'd said before: 'I gave him all the money. I gave him everything.'

'I know,' I nodded and his hands opened and closed as though they were the only part of his body that could speak any more. And then the woman who had tried to breathe life back into James came and hugged his mother and hugged me and led away the owner. And, lastly, the woman from the library came and held our hands and said nothing because there was nothing to say.

I thought about this for a long time and when I looked up George had left, slipping quietly away, leaving us to our separate and united grief. And a while later James's mother got up and opened the back door and went out into the garden and I heard her moving between the drills and the raised beds and I knew, without looking, that she was pulling everything from the ground, every living thing. I heard the glass crack in the little greenhouse by the end wall; I heard the sunflower stalks snap and then I heard her breath, coming heavy as she tugged their roots from the earth; I heard her sobs and I knew she was on her knees near the fence, that her face was pressed against the hard, dry earth. And I knew, of course I knew, that she had always been a good woman and that our son had been a good and beautiful boy and that I had tried to be a good man, but I understood, too, that goodness is not always enough.

The Water of Life

Ariana hired a car at the airport and they drove out of the city. Her father had been confused and irritable on the flight but she'd expected that. Her brother had told her she was crazy to take their father back.

'Either he'll remember nothing and it'll be a wasted journey, or he'll remember everything and there'll be mayhem.'

She hadn't had the energy to respond. Instead, she had gone ahead and booked the flights, the car, the hotel halfway between the airport and the town which was their destination, the place in which her father had grown up, and when the day had come she collected her father, took him to the airport and got them both on the plane.

Now that they were clear of the airport and out on the open, desert road, she felt more relaxed, more in control of the situation. Her father was dozing beside her, the light wind already tanning his face. She envied him that ability to change, chameleon-like, from pale to sallow to dark skin in a very short time. With her it was different; she was either pale or burnt. She never seemed to get beyond that point, could never look in the mirror and admire a tanned face.

She drove fast, the top down on the car, the warm breeze lifting her hair, the sun angling in above the windscreen, the desert stretching to the edges of the world on either side.

'What happens if you break down in the desert?' her brother had asked.

'I ring the car hire company.'

'And meantime you're stuck in the sand with a lunatic, not knowing what's going on in his mind or when he may flip. Rather you than me, girl.'

She hated the way he referred to her as girl, as though she were a child, as though all knowledge, rather than an abdication of every responsibility, lay with him and she knew nothing. Out here, for now at least, with her father sleeping, the sun shining and the car moving smoothly along the empty desert road, she could put her brother out of her mind and sit back, hands on the wheel, losing herself in the moment.

She had driven for over an hour before her father woke and, when he did, he looked quietly across the blanket of sand. She wasn't sure if he was confused by the landscape or quietly taking it in, and she didn't ask. Suffice that he was quiet and calm and that he hadn't reacted as her brother had predicted. They drove on, occasionally passing a lorry or car going in the opposite direction.

'I used to sit in the back of Peter's pick-up truck,' her father said quietly, his voice barely rising above the passing breeze. 'Bit like this but not as smooth. Him and me were the mature ones. Thomas the Elder he called me.'

She smiled and nodded, glancing at her father. He was smiling too.

'I always liked the desert,' he said. 'Always felt safer out here. You can see people coming in the desert, no surprises. Towns are full of surprises. But deserts are calm places.'

'Would you like to stop for a while, walk on the sand?'

'That'd be nice.'

She eased the car off the road and brought it to a gentle halt on the yellow grains.

'Peter always raised a storm,' her father said. 'We used to call the truck the Tornado. All you saw was this cloud of sand racing across the desert and us dancing like fish on hooks in the back.'

They stepped out of the car and she watched her father walk fifty paces into the desert. She was amazed at how dirty the sand was on each side of the road. Strewn with cigarette packs, plastic containers, paper, beer cans. But once you got twenty yards from the tar, it became clear and clean, stretching like yellow water out to the place where the sky came down to suck it back into the blue above.

She followed him out to where he was standing, beyond the mess that other people had left, and they stood together looking into a haze of heat.

'Are you glad to be back?' she asked.

'There was a place, somewhere out there.' His hand indicated a place that might have been anywhere in the shimmer that was this terrain. 'A ruined house that we camped near sometimes in summer. There was a man who used to come to the ruin every Saturday morning. Never knew why. We'd see him drive up in his Jeep, get out and spend some time in the shambles of fallen walls. He was a middle-aged man, respectable and well-dressed. Never spoke to us. Sometimes he'd wave in our direction, sometimes not. He had to have a reason for going back regularly to that place but we were never sure. Someone said something had happened to him in that place, in his youth. Someone had been killed, his girl or sister or brother. No one was sure, just these rumours that you get floating around out here in the dust storms. Somewhere out there.'

Again, he indicated the hundred miles of sand, as if hoping the ruined house would suddenly emerge from the mist and prove that what he was saying was true.

'That's sad,' his daughter said.

He nodded and then smiled.

'But maybe he was thinking about buying the place and there was no tragedy. Maybe it was all just talk, like your brother goes on with.'

She smiled and his smile broadened to a grin.

'I'm glad he didn't come,' he said. 'Things will be better without him, for both of us.'

'You could be right.'

He turned away again and walked a short distance into the desert. She stayed where she was and watched the figure who was her father but might have been anyone move slowly against the skyline. For a while, she thought he was going to continue walking but then he stopped and became a frozen icon in the burning air. He stayed like that for a long time – staring into something or at something – she wasn't sure which, until, finally, he turned and walked back towards her.

'I love this dry heat,' he said, sitting back into the car. 'I could have lived with that.'

'It's pleasant.'

'Cold out here at night but you can prepare for the cold.'

She started the engine and pulled back onto the open road.

'One time,' her father said, 'I was driving this road or one like it and I saw a car pulled over by the roadside. A woman waved me down, so I stopped. She was a psychologist. Said her car had let her down. I sat in and turned the key and it started immediately. She was very cool about the whole thing, just shrugged and said, "Seems I've just had a mental breakdown."'

He laughed raucously and his daughter glanced at him. It took a moment for her to realise he was laughing at his own joke. Jokes made her nervous. Sometimes she didn't get them and felt foolish. But this was the first time in almost two years that her father had told a joke. Humour had slipped away with memory, to be replaced by frustration and anger.

'You were never very fond of humour,' her father said. 'But that's not a crime.'

'No.'

'The thing about forgetting is that sometimes it's frustrating but sometimes it's a good thing to forget.'

'Has the desert brought back memories? Are you finding this tough?'

'No,' he said. 'It's okay. I'm okay. You and me are okay, aren't we?'

'We are,' she smiled. 'Yes we are.'

The following morning, after breakfast in the motel where she'd hardly slept, worrying in case her father might wander from his room, Ariana packed their bags in the car and they set off the twenty miles that would take them to the town she had been hearing about for as long as she could remember.

He was quieter today. No jokes and no conversation.

'We'll be there in half an hour,' she said.

She thought she saw him wince.

'Are you okay?'

He pursed his lips and nodded.

'We don't have to do this, you know,' Ariana said. 'We can just drive up the coast, stop off at some of the little fishing villages. We can relax and enjoy the heat. This is not meant to be a penance.'

Her father laughed, a dry, humourless laugh and she regretted saying anything.

Gradually the desert skyline became a mirage of forms that slowly focused into the shapes of factories and then apartment blocks and houses.

She drove slowly through the streets, conscious that her father might want to find his emotional bearings.

'This is it?' he asked.

'Yes, this is it.'

'It's different.'

'More than twenty years different. I'm sure the centre of the town won't have changed all that much. Suburbs are always the first to change.'

'And we'll find the well?'

'I'm sure we'll find the well.'

Just as jokes frightened Ariana, certainty also frightened her. She was loath to promise her father that they would definitely find a well that had been a central part of the town more than twenty years before but might now have been capped and lost.

They drove slowly into what the map said was the old part of the town but there were roundabouts and one-way streets in every direction.

'Looks like we may have to walk,' she said, finally.

'I don't remember any of this,' her father said. Already there were sweat stains beneath the arms of his shirt. 'This is not the way it used to be. It used to be just four or five streets. I knew every shop. You sure we're in the right place?'

'We'll park,' Ariana said. 'We'll park at the top of this street, if we can, and we'll walk. You okay to walk?'

Her father nodded but she could see that he was restless and confused. She cursed herself for not checking the place out beforehand. She had heard her father's stories so often that she had allowed herself to believe things would be as he remembered them. But it was obvious that they weren't. It was evident that the whole town had been redesigned and realigned in the past twenty years.

Swinging the car into a side street, she found a parking space. It took her longer than she had expected to get the roof up and to get her father out and walking. He was moving slowly now. The energy of the day before was gone but he was still lucid.

They walked on the shaded side of the narrow street and when they reached the corner she read the names of the streets that arrowed in from the left and right.

'Swan Street and April Street. Lovely names. Do you remember them?'

Her father shook his head.

'They changed a lot of the names after the revolution.'

'Right.'

She looked to the left and right but there was no one to be seen on the streets.

'Let's find some place to eat, have a coffee, make enquiries. That all right with you?'

'Yes.'

'We'll try this way.'

They turned right onto April Street, still in the shade of the buildings, and walked until they found a small café. They sat outside and Ariana ordered two cappuccinos. When the waiter brought the coffees, she asked him about the old town and if he knew where they might find the well.

'No wells around here,' the waiter shrugged.

'It might be covered now. It was here twenty years ago.'

He shook his head.

'No wells. No, no wells. I would know.'

'Joseph's Well?'

The waiter shrugged her question away.

'Absolutely no wells here.'

'There were a thousand fucking wells,' her father said, rising from his chair. 'Every street, every square, every courtyard had a well. Don't stand there and tell us there are no wells. This town is built on wells.'

'It's all right,' Ariana said, easing him back into his chair. 'It's okay. We'll find it.'

'No wells – do you take us for idiots?' her father shouted at the waiter, who shrugged again and walked away with a look of disdain on his face.

Ariana sipped her coffee while her father fumed quietly.

'Fuckhead,' he said finally. 'It's my memory that's going, not my mind. I'll bet that asshole hasn't been in this town for more than a couple of months. That's not a local accent. Prick.'

Ariana smiled.

'There are a lot of words you haven't mislaid.'

Her father smiled, too, and sipped his coffee.

'No, no wells. I would know,' he mimicked the waiter. 'I hope he falls down the deepest one there is and drowns.'

'Charming,' Ariana said.

It was almost lunchtime before they found the place where the ancient walls had stood, the area where the square and the well should have been. An old woman took them there and stood with them on the side of a busy four-lane road.

'This is where it was,' she said.

'They put a road through it?' Ariana's father asked.

'Yes. Maybe twelve, fifteen years ago.'

'Do you remember the square, the well?' Ariana asked.

The old woman looked at her suspiciously.

'Those were different times,' she said. 'Best left, best forgotten.'

'We're not secret police,' Ariana's father said.

The woman looked at him, staring into his eyes, and seemed to accept that he was telling the truth.

'I remember,' she said.

'Do you remember the Captain?' he asked.

The old woman went pale and seemed about to faint. James reached out quickly and took her arm to steady her. Ariana looked at the elderly pair standing before her – one weak and shocked, one gradually losing his mind – and she saw two people to whom that man had meant so much.

'Yes, I remember the Captain,' the old woman said and she didn't try to loosen James's grip on her arm. 'He was a good man. You were one of his comrades?'

'Yes.'

'It was a dark time.'

'Yes.'

'And you have come back to revisit the old places?' she asked formally.

'Yes.'

'They have buried everything they could bury – roads and offices and car parks built on the old places. But they cannot bury the memories.'

'No,' the old man said, 'they can't bury the memories. Only we can do that.'

'You were one of his comrades?' the woman asked again.

'Yes.'

'One of the close ones?'

'Yes.'

The old woman stepped away from James, then reached out and touched the side of his face with the palm of her hand. There were tears in her eyes but she said nothing, just turned and walked slowly away.

Ariana and her father stood in the bright sunlight until the old woman disappeared around a corner and out of their lives.

'Would you like to sit down?'

He nodded.

Ariana guided him to a low wall by the roadside and they sat together.

'It was out there,' her father said, indicating the roadway. 'Wherever it was. There was a square with a well in the middle. We came here one evening late and he and I sat at the well, waiting for the others to come back with food, and this woman, this Samarian woman, came to draw water and she and the Captain fell into a conversation about politics and life and death. He talked to her about the living water and I could see that she thought he was crazy and yet she was drawn to what he was saying. And I was drawn to her. She was so, so beautiful. I think, had she asked, I'd have followed her that night. But she didn't.'

'I might have grown up here if you had,' Ariana smiled.

'And I might be back here now, looking for you, having fled all those years ago,' her father said. 'I'm glad that didn't happen. To have lost you....'

The sentence remained unfinished, as though the thought or the words to express the thought had disappeared, evaporating before he could shape or speak them.

She put her hand on his and his fist closed about her fingers, squeezing tightly. She saw that there were tears running down his face, perhaps for the Captain, perhaps for the Samarian woman, perhaps for himself, most likely for all of them or for something half-remembered.

'I don't think we should stay here,' her father said that evening as they ate dinner.

'Here, in this hotel? Or here, in this town?'

'This town.'

'It's changed.'

'It's not just changed; it's been changed.'

'Yes. It seems like it has.'

'We should go tomorrow.'

'All right.'

That night, she heard him pacing the room next door, heard him turn the TV on and off and on and off again. Once she thought she heard his door open and she rushed into the corridor but there was no one there. Daylight was kissing her bedroom window before she slept and three hours later she was eating breakfast with her father.

'We have a day to kill,' Ariana said. 'We can drive up the coast, if you'd like, then drive back through the desert to the airport on Thursday.'

Her father thought about this for a moment.

'Yes,' he said. 'Yes.'

They drove slowly up the coastal road, the sea breezes rinsing their skin.

For a long time Ariana wondered if she should say what was on her mind. The miles and the villages passed but the sea was a constant on their left-hand side, dipping and troughing in the sunlight, the blue deepening while the sun rose through the morning sky.

They stopped for lunch at a restaurant overlooking a harbour. On the sand, below the harbour wall, a trawler lay on its side, the broken hull flooded with damp sand. Halfway through the meal, it seemed to catch her father's attention and he laughed.

'Looks like the charred remains of all the boats I've burned.'

And those were the last words he spoke that day. The afternoon and evening passed in silence. Whenever his daughter spoke, he either stared blankly or ignored her. He was silent through dinner and silent when she bade him goodnight. She tried to stay awake but she couldn't and by the time she woke the following morning he was already in the motel restaurant.

'Did you sleep all right?'

'Yes,' he said, returning immediately to his coffee and fruit.

She remembered the first time, after the diagnosis, that they had been together alone. She had driven with him, out to a cricket pitch near the town where he lived. It was a warm, damp September morning and two men were dragging a roller up and down the wicket, its weight bending the short grass and flattening the earth. They had sat on a bench overlooking the pitch and her father had dozed in the early autumn sun. A tear had finally trickled down her face and he had woken and asked her why she was crying and she had answered that she didn't know.

'Is it because I'm disappearing?' he had asked.

And then the tears had come in sweeps, one flooding after the other, and her father had put his arm around her and held her until the spasms slowed and slowed and finally stopped.

Later that morning, driving back through the desert, he said: 'Maybe that's why I'm forgetting, because there's too much to remember.'

'Is it odd for you,' she asked, 'the way things come and go? Memory. Vocabulary. Emotions.'

'Sometimes I don't know what's happening. It's like stepping off a chair and finding it's really a cliff. And sometimes it's just stepping off the chair – those are the worst times because I want to stay on the chair but I can't and that makes me angry. And sometimes it doesn't matter because everything is gone. But the things start coming back. Like this morning: I woke up and I knew everything. I knew you were sleeping and I knew I could go and have my breakfast. I recognised the present and I could remember the past.'

She waited for him to say more but he didn't.

They drove on in silence, the small waves of sand lapping the roadside, the sun rising hot and strong, its shape and colour becoming less focused as it burned its way through the rising morning sky. And then the road began to climb, up towards the pale hot sun, arcing and twisting along the edge of a mountain, the sand turning to rock, the road a rough, black runner coiling back on itself, hugging the edges of cliffs before sweeping away, only to return again to the precipice.

Mid-morning they stopped in the shadows of a ruined village and Ariana took some water and food from a cooler bag. They walked through the broken, roofless houses until they found a comfortable place to sit, shaded and not too hot, looking out over the barren valley. They ate and drank in silence and afterwards her father walked to the edge of the cliff and stretched slowly in the sunlight. Then he turned and walked back to where she was sitting.

'They say you can see the bullet that kills you,' he said.

'Do they?'

'So I've heard.'

'I suppose there's no way of proving or disproving it,' she smiled.

'True.'

He looked around the ruined walls of the house that sheltered them from the brilliance of the sun.

'It was a place a bit like this.'

'What was?'

'The house where we took the Captain's body, after the ambush. It was bigger than this and not on a mountain but the same stone, same....' He paused, searching for a word. 'Design, layout, shape. Same shape.'

'Right.'

'But it was a lot bigger. We often had twenty people staying there.'

'Yes.'

'There were eight or ten of us there after he died. Seemed to be the safest place to go. It was safer than the town. Anywhere was safer than the town.'

'Yes.'

'That's where we buried him, in the desert, Peter and myself. The others had gone by then. Scattered. Terrified. Peter was a good man. Some people thought he was too short-tempered, too brusque. I thought he was straight-talking but kind.'

'Was he the one you liked best?'

Her father nodded and then he was silent again.

'And the Captain?'

'Ah, the Captain was a different story. Every time he went somewhere, you felt like everything was gone. You couldn't wait for him to come back again. Of course we didn't know then that things would end the way they did. We knew we were in danger but we never in our wildest dreams expected him to be shot down on the road. Maybe he expected something like that, but not the rest of us.'

'Maybe he did.'

'Isn't it better to have your sins forgotten than to have them forgiven?'

Ariana thought for a moment, not sure whether he expected an answer. He glanced at his wristwatch.

'You want to get going again?' she asked.

'You're the driver.'

'We probably should.'

They walked back down through the rubbled alleyways, between the falling walls, and she smiled at her father's sureness of foot. His mind might stumble but his feet never would.

They were an hour from the airport when he spoke again.

'I have three beds in three different houses.'

'Do you?'

'Your brother is a right little prick. He's a bully.'

'Yes, I've noticed.'

The distant sky was criss-crossed with the vapour trails of incoming and outgoing planes. The signs put her on the road to the drop-off point for the car. Planes roared just above them.

'Almost there,' she shouted.

Her father didn't seem to be listening. She glanced across at him. There were tears flowing down his face.

'Are you all right?' she asked.

For a moment, he didn't speak and when he did his voice was low and dark but she caught his words between the snarls of the aeroplane engines.

'I have nowhere to hide when I'm afraid. And the strange thing is that I'm lost most of the time.'

'I'll look after you. I won't let you get lost, I promise,' she said gently, but something drowned out her voice, something far harsher than the aircraft engines, and her father went on crying.

Once We Sang Like Other Men

The same few songs have been playing all summer. I've hated some of them since the first time I heard them and some have grown on me. Some days they remind me of Andrew, sitting on the porch of the house that was home, playing his harmonica. Not the kind of music, just the fact that it's there, as a constant, the way his harmonica is a constant in my memory of that time and that place.

Laz died in the early part of last summer and this time there was no coming back, and I'm glad. And I have no doubt but that he was glad too. He just died, in his chair. I was out on the boat, taking two Americans on a fishing trip. When I got back, I checked that he was in his chair, same as I always did. Waved even. He didn't wave back but there was nothing new in that. Sometimes he was asleep, sometimes he just couldn't be bothered, sometimes he didn't have the strength. I scrubbed the deck, just to be ready for the next outing, did a quick tidy around the boat, replaced an oil filter, the usual bits and pieces. It was a sunny evening, clear skies and warm. When the work was done, I rambled down to the corner shop and picked up some stuff for our supper and something for breakfast and then rambled back here. Same as I've done a hundred evenings.

I have no idea how long he'd been gone; it could have been minutes and it could have been hours; it doesn't matter. The doctor came and later the undertaker and we prepared him for burial, put him in a box and nailed him down. Two and a half decades he'd lasted and I'd reckon there was something between eighty and a hundred days in all that time that you could say he was truly happy. And, if he was here, he might have added another fifty days in his life up to that, four or five months' happiness in sixty years. It seems to me he was one of those people for whom life is a series of traps laid in the most unexpected places but, unlike most people, even one death wasn't enough to save him from suffering.

Near the end, I'd hear him swearing more than usual. Muttering, when I could understand him, that he wished he were dead and that they'd left him be the first time, trying to catch his breath, sobbing. I knew he was distressed. I was distressed myself by what was going on but I didn't realise he was dying.

After the doctor and the undertaker had done their work, I rang his sisters to tell them. Martha answered.

'It needn't have been this way,' she said.

'You're right,' I said. 'He could have died years ago on the side of the street with a stupid fucking cardboard placard around his neck and a begging bowl in his lap.'

'You have no faith,' she said in that sanctimonious tone I hate.

'I think I know that. I think everybody knows that,' I said and then I hung up.

She called me back later that afternoon. She said her sister and herself had been talking things over and they wanted to bury Laz back home. So the following morning the undertaker and myself drove to the nearest railway station, put the coffin on the train and sent him on his way.

I waited two weeks for a call from Martha and then I called her.

'He had a lovely send off,' she said. 'But it was all so different from the first time he died, so different this time. We miss the Captain. Even now.'

I thought she was taking the piss but she wasn't. And then the crocodile tears started.

I missed him for a while, missed him sitting in his throne chair, missed the odd days when he was up to talking. I was going to throw the wheelchair away. Good thing I didn't – waste not, want not.

I had intended throwing it into the sea as a kind of symbolic farewell to Laz, something to do in the absence of a funeral. One afternoon, about a week after I'd shipped him home, I folded it up and put it in the boat. I thought I'd take it out that evening and drop it off the Point but the weather turned and a squall blew up so I couldn't take Treetop out. The following day I had some tourists to bring on a fishing trip and I thought it best not to leave the wheelchair lying on the deck, so I stored it in a corner at the back of the workshop and forgot about it and there it stayed. Which is a good thing, or will be, and, of course, I didn't know then what I know now.

I did have some sense that something was wrong, that things weren't working as they should have been. It was a feeling that just seemed to grow over a period of months. Looking back, there were signs even before Laz died, little things like losing my balance, stuff like that. There and gone. He'd laugh and tell me I was drunk and I'd laugh too because sometimes he might have been right. It got worse after he died, just for a couple of weeks, and I put that down to stress. There was lots of stress about. Trying to make a living, Laz's death, shipping him home, a letter from my wife, half of it berating me for never having come back – she'd got my address from Martha once word got out that Laz was dead or dead again. The other half telling me she'd like me to come back. I didn't reply. I saw no point. Too much time had passed, too much was happening inside me, even if I didn't know why. I wasn't going to crawl back like a sick animal looking for somewhere clean to die.

For a couple of months after that, every time I saw the morning or evening bus squeal to a halt on the town square, I expected to see my wife get off it. And that got me thinking about Andrew and missing him and wondering if he was alive or dead. So I blamed a lot of things that were happening on stress.

But, deep down, I think knew there was something else going on and going wrong. The loss of balance, the dizziness, the times when I'd tell my limbs what to do but they'd refuse to behave, the difficulties in swallowing, the not being able to dock the boat as well and as quickly as I used to.

One of the other boatmen shouted at me one evening, laughing: 'You're losing the knack.'

I laughed, too, but I knew he was right. I had only to look at how I'd tied her up to know how right he was.

They tell me it'll be two to three years before it takes full effect. So Laz's chair will be useful then. The Doc tells me it'll do me for a time. 'But there'll come a day when you won't be able to move, we'll need to find you a place somewhere – you'll need full-time care. But we'll face that when the time comes. In the meantime we'll keep you as well as we can.'

He's a decent bloke. I bring him fish on Fridays. He doesn't charge me for his services and I don't charge him for mine.

So, when the time comes, there'll be someone there to feed me, change my clothes, wipe my arse, walk me and turn me and see me out of this world at the end.

And in the meantime Laz's chair will come in useful.

Early this summer, someone did get off the evening bus, someone I recognised from years before. Not my wife and not the Captain reincarnated and not one of the band of men with whom I once sang around the campfire.

I was sitting here, just after seven on a fine sunny evening, sipping my coffee and listening to the music coming from the bar across the square and then the bus came sweeping in, as it always does in the evening, the driver doing his handbrake stop across the sanded square, grinding to a skidding halt outside the newsagents. I heard the door creak open and, a few seconds later, I heard it creak closed again and then the bus moved away, in another storm of sand, and eventually, when the dust had settled, I saw the figure of a woman standing outside the shop, a rucksack at her feet, hair tied back, face tanned. I knew, immediately, instinctively, that it was Katy. She was squinting into the sun, trying to get her bearings, and when she saw me sitting here, at the other end of the short street that runs off the square and down to the quay, she smiled and waved, as though we'd parted just the week before.

The years had been kind to her. She was still just a young woman, forty-seven or forty-eight, no more than that, still as beautiful.

I walked up to meet her, coffee cup in hand, stunned yet completely pleased by her arrival. I didn't stumble, I didn't fall, every ache and symptom had disappeared, every fibre in my body and my brain was focused on her.

She stayed for eighteen days.

We went out on the boat, we ate in the local cafés, I showed her the sights, such as they are, and we drove up the coast. She laughed when she saw the pick-up, the same pick-up I'd had a quarter of a century before.

'Still the dreamer,' she said and I nodded. 'Strange to sit where he sat.'

I thought of Crystal Gayle and 'Crying in the Rain' but I didn't mention it because I didn't want to risk discovering that she'd forgotten that night.

We talked about the Captain's father. Katy told me he was still alive.

'Must be a hell of an age,' I said.

'He is but he's still sprightly, still as sharp as a razor. Looks after himself.'

I asked if she'd kept in contact with anyone else from the old days. She said she hadn't. She told me she'd heard about Laz's death and she'd found me through Martha.

'You're not the only one,' I said.

She didn't ask for an explanation.

We were sitting in the pick-up when Katy asked me to tell her what had happened when we took the Captain's body into the desert. We were parked on a lay-by, looking out over the sea, on a cliff twenty miles up the coast from here. So I told her. I told her the truth.

'You remember, that night, after we took his body from the hospital? You brought his father to the other safe house.'

She nodded.

'Some time during that night, during the wake, someone mentioned what the Captain had said at the last meal we'd had together. I know you weren't there. I don't know if you know what happened?'

'I've heard the rumours but I'd like to hear the truth from someone who was there.'

'We were eating – nothing unusual in that. It was just another meal but then he took some bread and broke it and he held it in his hand and said: "This is my body, take it and eat." And a moment later he raised his wine glass and said: "This is my blood; it will be shed for you."'

I was silent, waiting for her to say something but she didn't. I knew she was looking at me but I kept my eyes fixed on the trawler ploughing its way through the choppy waters.

'It was strange that night because we weren't sure about what we were hearing. When he spoke, we listened, you know how that was, Katy. You know the gift he had for words; you were there most of the time to hear them, to see him work the crowds. You know how he read poetry all the time and how so much of what he said came out in riddles and images that were like poems. That night, at the meal, we'd taken his words as a poem, as a metaphor, a dark one but a metaphor nevertheless. And when he passed the bread and wine around the table, we ate it and we drank from the glass and there was a sense that we were part of something true. It felt like we were being made a promise that would be kept. But nothing more than that. In spite of the fact that there was a sense of imminent doom, for those few minutes it was like the early days again. There was almost a giddiness about us.'

I looked at her, held her gaze for a moment and then looked back at the sea, finding the trawler, using it as something on which to concentrate.

'In the house, after he'd been shot, we got around to talking about what he'd said at the meal. We knew he'd sensed the danger, we all had, that they really were coming for him this time and that no stone would be left unturned to bring the movement to an end. I think he understood how it all would happen, that they wouldn't bother with an arrest or the pretence of a trial, that it would be easier and cleaner to go for the immediate execution. It was happening to others, so why not to him? The only things he didn't know were where and when. But you know all this.'

Out of the corner of my eye, I caught a slight movement of her head and I took it as assent.

'So, that night, while we sat with his body, we talked and we kept coming back to the words, the only things we had left of him. And someone wondered, tentatively at first, if he'd been talking literally, if this was the message he'd left for us, if he'd given us the answer but we hadn't had the foresight to recognise it. Whether it was the wine or fear or hope or hopelessness, we took his body into the desert and we did what he had told us to do. We ate the bread and we drank his wine.'

I waited for her to react, but no reaction came.

'Do you know what I'm telling you? I'm telling you what happened. We did what he told us to do, Katy. We ate his flesh and we drank his blood. And then we waited for the miracle to happen until, slowly, it dawned on us that there wasn't going to be a miracle, that the Captain wasn't coming back and the whole thing was over. And then the enormity of what we'd done started to sink in and we were horrified, guilt-ridden, and the unspoken blame began. We dared not look at each other. Discussing it was never an issue because we couldn't. James and myself buried what was left of the Captain's body in the desert. No words, no ceremony, no songs, no poetry, just an act of necessity. Matt and Andy were the first to leave. I woke one morning and they were gone. Within a week the rest had scattered. I was the last to go. I wanted to say or do something to bring things to a close; I felt I owed him that. So I went down, just as the sun was rising, on my last day at the house, and stood at the spot where we had buried him. We'd put four large stones in a line along the lie of the grave. I took them and hurled each one as far as I could across the red morning sand, one towards each of the compass points so that, even if we wanted to, we could never find his burial place again. And then I drove for three days, stopping only to fill the petrol tank, living on coffee, driving without any sleep. On the third night, on the outskirts of some one-horse town, I thought I saw the Captain walking on the hard shoulder and my heart sang and I could feel the blood rushing in my ears and I slowed the pick-up and stopped but there was no one there; of course there was no one there. I was hallucinating, I needed sleep. So I pulled over the pick-up and I closed my eyes and I slept for thirteen hours and then I got on with the rest of my life.'

We were both silent for a long, long time. The trawler ploughed on across the horizon, heading for God knew where. And then, at last, Katy spoke.

'And you never thought make contact? You just disappeared out of my life.'

'How could I tell you?' I asked. 'I've never spoken of it to anyone before today. I never will again.'

She said nothing. I took her hand and held it and, eventually, she touched the side of her face with the back of my hand. She had never been a smiler but now she smiled, a small delicate smile that was there and then was gone.

A few nights later she took me dancing. We made love. I told her about this stuff that's coming down the line, this thing that's eating into my body, this thing that will make a sick joke of my life. And she said it was okay. She said: 'We'll deal with it when it comes.'

But that wasn't what I wanted her to say; that wasn't what I wanted to hear. The last thing I could face was Katy's sympathy. I had got this far alone. I had lived with the memory and the guilt and the loss for twenty-five years and I wasn't going to be carried the rest of the way. Ungrateful? Perhaps. Stubborn? Certainly. Proud? Absolutely.

In the end, I insisted she leave. I gave her reasons why she should go. I made excuses as to why she couldn't stay. I may even have told her I was thinking of going home. She knew I was lying but she knew, too, that I couldn't bear to have her stay and see me disintegrate.

So we made love one last time and the following morning I walked her to the bus stop and we stood together in the dusty square and the bus skidded to a halt in a blur of dust and, as it did, I told her to do the things she needed to do and go to the places she wanted to go.

'I thought I had,' she said.

I shook my head.

'Well, there you go,' she said and then she stepped onto the bus and the door closed and she was gone.

And, in that instant, as the bus pulled off, I realised that I had made a mistake, that I was wrong to send her away. I was wrong. And, after everything, that is the greatest regret of my life. Just that. But there's no going back.

Acknowledgements

A very sincere thank you to Richard Ball, who planted the seed; to Pierce Pettis and the late Leonard Cohen for permission to use their lyrics; to Sinead Dowling, Carlow County Council Arts Officer and everyone at Carlow County Council Arts Office for their support and to Jonathan Williams for his unfailing enthusiasm and encouragement.